Foreword

In writing this book I spent hours writing and toying with the idea of whether this work should be fiction or nonfiction, for those who know me in real life you will notice that this book follows a lot of my timeline, it is based on my life, I've chosen to add some details, to change names, and to convert it to fiction to preserve the rights of those closest to me, and to also preserve the privacy of myself, so if you find yourself wondering if this is my life story-keep wondering. I've written this book because we've all been through so many things in life, many women and men find themselves struggling with alcohol or drugs and not knowing how to cope so it's my hope to share hope, faith, and encourage each and every one of you to not give up. I dedicate this book to my non-stop inspiration, my non-stop encourager of the truth future husband Sunil, and also to two special someone in my life Daniel and Snow who may not be always on speaking terms or understanding the things I do but I hope one day in the future they'll know and understand it all.

Birth to Toddler

Hi, My name is Britney Christine Thomas- I was born on Thursday, March 24, 1988, around 930 AM in the morning in Nampa, Idaho, I was born with crooked legs to the parents of Ester Jo Thomas and Colin Marion Thomas, I was the youngest sibling and the only girl, I had 3 older brothers. When I was 1 month old, my parents took a gigantic risk and moved us from Idaho to Mississippi with no job, no home lined up, only hope and faith it would work out.

Growing up in Mississippi I loved to dance and read, I would spend hours as a 3 and 4-year-old reading book after book, dancing in the mirror, and when I was scared the safest place was near my dad. When I was 4 I had a traumatic event happen to me and I learned without realizing that I could make myself block out things. At the age of 5, I began Elementary school and my first teacher's name was Mrs. Name, she taught us all kinds of things including how to spell the word Mississippi "MI crooked letter crooked letter I crooked letter I humpback I" I made 2 friends and I was a happy girl. I loved to smile and read and dance.

In December 1993 my parents had saved enough money to buy land in Alabama, and they made a down payment on a trailer, we started the process of moving there. My dad let me sit with him on the bulldozer, and we got to watch as they removed enough trees to create a spot for our new trailer- I still have these vivid memories of piles of trees and my mom and dad telling us we all have to pitch in.. soon after we as a family began digging the hole for our well, the ditch to lay the pipes to get water from our well to our house, digging hole after hole to set up our fence, planting grass, planting flowers, my father believed in the necessity of us knowing how to create things, build things, and hard work. We moved into our trailer right before Christmas in 1993, I was nervous to be starting a new school in January, but also excited. Christmas, as usual, was both happy and upsetting my mom usually spent half the day excited they taught me the beauty of making Christmas special- of having the innocence of imagination, they kept me believing in Santa Clause until I was about 7 years old. But whether it was my mom being tired or just stressed over money by noon she usually got angry and would retreat to her room for a nap leaving my dad to hang out with me and my brothers. It was a special day, New years that year and most years meant something low key, getting to stay up till midnight to celebrate the new year, if my parents were especially happy they would share some champagne but mostly my dad was the only one who would drink.

Elementary School

The New year came about and it was time for me to start at Wilmer Elementary School, I was in 1st grade and my teachers name was Mrs. Coleman, she was an intimidating presence on the exterior and my first day I spent in tears, I was scared and didn't know anyone, my brother Chris was starting in his new 3rd grade classroom but he always made friends easily- or just started fights but he promised to watch out for me so away I went to class. That day we got to go to the computer lab and play the Oregon Trail game, it was amazing and as soon as I got home from school that day I asked dad if we could install it on our computer- we had just changed over from DOS to a Windows computer and I wanted to play it. I didn't have to wait long and I soon began my adventures on the Oregon Trail fighting diseases, dysentery, infections, and soon after that, I began making friends. The school was an interesting place but I soon found my click with some girls that lived nearby and two of them rode the same school bus as me though one lived on the other side of the neighborhood that I wasn't allowed to go to at first.

Our friendships began, I would often go and stay the night at my best friend Candace's house, and sometimes her and my other best friend Nikita would come to stay at my house, we gathered more friends and had weekly sleepovers, dancing in our pajamas, going to church on the weekends on the church bus, and just having fun as young girls. Around the time we hit Second grade we began discovering the wonderful world of rap music- Sir Mix a lot was the rapper to listen to- we learned it was good to have big butts and skinny waists, we created our choreography to "Big butts" and would spend recess dancing to it on the playground, we discovered that girls should have boyfriends and we set out to get one. We all found boys to like and eventually started having our first boyfriends- which at that time just meant we were friends with a boy. Second grade in itself meant making new friends, having yet more sleepovers, campouts, attending church, volunteering to sing in pageants, trying out for the talent show, and having fun. My brother Chris was getting angrier and struggling more with behavior issues and he was often in trouble for fighting. I was the good kid, my other brothers were in my mom's eyes often useless, they were her step kids and she didn't have the greatest bond with them and they didn't make it easier for her, they often stole her stuff, talked back, and were disrespectful.

Third grade came and with it, I discovered the benefits of helping teachers, volunteering to be of assistance to them I was a "suck up" and I have no issues with it, I would be the kid volunteering to help grade papers, organize things, pass out papers, I enjoyed being a good girl. My home life was often chaotic my brothers always acted up, I just wanted to study, to read, to make good grades, and I stayed with my friends as often as I could where we would eat mass amounts of candy, stay up all night, and play board games. In 4th grade I had one of the meanest teachers in the school she was known as the teacher to give detentions first and ask questions later- she hated my brother having had him a few years previously but my brother was off to 6th grade and I made it my mission to have a teacher like me. I volunteered to help her, I worked hard, I volunteered in the special education classroom, and I made straight A's. She loved me and I was one of the first students to be called on to answer questions or to help her, when Halloween came she asked me to help create the class themed haunted house and I got to spend hours with her and my best friend Nikita coming up with ideas of what to use as brains and eyeballs, how to create smoke, and make it spooky. It was such a fun time in my life, I had erased the past bad deeds of my brother Chris and I was an amazing student.

5th grade rolled along, it was my last year in elementary school, I had one of the highest reading levels in the grade, I was part of the 4-h club, student volunteer, teachers pet, I was aiming to be an Azalea trail made in high school, I knew what I wanted to be when I grew up (A doctor or psychiatrist) and I was on track. All my friends beside Nikita had discovered boys again with a vengeance and having older brothers meant they often wanted to spend time at my house where my parents were hosting parties for my brother Chris that meant he and his friends would get wasted. In my house, it was common to talk about sex, cocaine, weed, and alcohol, my parents were classified as cool parents, and I hated it, I spent all my time with friends that I could. I hated alcohol and its smell, I hated how it made my brother and his friends act. They scared me. My dad was usually in the mix of it high on cocaine, my mom would be smoking weed, and I would be hiding in my room with my door locked waiting till everyone passed out. I stayed sane by planning out what my friend Nikita and I would make for our teachers, we would spend hours practicing cooking at her house, or we would hop on my 4-wheeler, or go riding on horses, anything to escape home. We also loved to swim so we would either drive the four-wheeler the 3 miles to the river to swim or we would go in my swimming pool. 5th grade was coming to a close, I had tried out for the band and was going to start playing the clarinet in 6th grade, I was on the honor roll, and I got to attend the 5th-grade dance with a date who happened to be a best friend. It was a fun time, soon after I got a job babysitting my other friend's brother and sister as she had gotten sent away to live with her dad because she was too promiscuous for her mom to handle, and I saved up enough money to buy roller skates and a boom box.

I spent the Summer of 1999 babysitting, getting my routine ready to try out to be a cheerleader in middle school, hanging with my friends, and tanning in the pool with friends. Fall of

1999 I tried out to be a cheerleader, I didn't make it, so I tried out to join the basketball team, got accepted but chose to instead join scholars bowl - I loved to answer questions like in jeopardy, and we got to leave the school often during the middle of the day. 6th grade was a myriad of emotions, all my friends from elementary school had changed during school, they were growing up and I seemed to be stuck as I was, confused, not yet a woman, but I made new friends, a new best friend and her, I, and Nikita would make food for our teachers, practice our clarinets, and go roller skating on the weekends. Life was fun, we spent our time doing homework, growing up, getting interested in boys, and preparing to take the SATS. 6th and 7th grade were pretty similar years. Clarinet practice, swimming in the pool, hanging out together, going to Mardi gras parades, having sleepovers, doing homework, I started writing dark poetry, and someone I knew eventually took their own life-middle school was hard. Emotions, peer pressure, sex, expectations were everywhere, I stayed true to who I was- a nerd. My brothers and family started calling me a fat girl and putting me down, so I started eating more, I retreated into my dark poetry and books, I would spend hours on the computer chatting with strangers, anything to get away from what was my real life.

The Spring of 2001 my dad was relocated to work for a time in New Jersey, my mom was smoking a lot of weed, my brother Chris was drinking, using meth, and weed, my older brother Ben had joined the Navy, and my other brother Oliver ran away to Alaska. So here I was this 11-year-old girl stuck in a house with a mom who was never home, a brother who was always high off his mind, and I had my second traumatic experience, and I had no one I could tell. So once again I learned how to block things out when my dad called I begged him to let me go live with him in New Jersey, but he wasn't able to at that time. My brother Chris drank more, smoked more, got into loud yelling matches with my mom, my mom when she was home would take to hit my brother, to this day I am still not certain why they fought so much, but eventually she kicked him out, yes she kicked a 14 year old boy out and he camped out in the woods. I would sneak him food and water while she was away getting high with her guy friend. Eventually a day came where she came home and realized she was missing food and she found him, they got into yet another fight, they were hitting each other so bad and I was standing there watching it, crying hysterically, I didn't know what to do, my dad was home for a visit and he got into the middle of it, him and my brother started punching each other so hard. My mom called the kids and the sheriff came, he arrested my brother telling him in this state we respect our elders and juvenile detention will teach him that. He got released a few days later with a stern warning, my dad flew back to Jersey, and my brother and mom started fighting more often only this time she pressed charges against her son. He went to jail. She went back to hanging out with her guy friend and I was alone in the house.

July of 2001 my mom was tired of taking care of my brother and me, and I was tired of being an adult I begged my dad to let us move in with him in Jersey, so we flew up to Jersey to live with my dad, my mom and him were talking divorce, we spent our nights eating pizza, I spent my days going to work with my dad, hanging with his coworkers kids at the beach, and started planning to attend my last year in middle school. 8th grade was the last year as a kid, the year before high school, the year when everything changes- I went to Woodbridge Middle School, my mom eventually came and lived with us, and I made friends.

My friends and I would spend hours walking around the mall, hanging out at houses, talking about boys, my best friend in Jersey and I would go to school early and volunteer to hang with our science teacher, we would spend hours in woodshop working on our rocking horses or gumball machines, and I joined the home economics class and learned proper baking techniques. September 2001 while sitting in history class the world trade centers were destroyed, it was a scary day and walking home from school knowing our classmates were being comforted was a surreal moment of knowing that life is scary and hard. In the winter of 2001 I rejoined band meanwhile my brother Chris had found new friends to drink and do drugs with, he had joined a gang and we would later learn he was in over his head. In January 2001 my parents made plans to go to Italy and I was sent to spend a few weeks with my best friend Nicole in Alabama. I was so excited we spent hours watching Buffy the Vampire Slayer, playing with candles, pretending to be witches, going roller skating, attending Mardi Gras parades and hockey games. It was the best 2 weeks of my 8th grade. When I returned from Alabama my brother had been beaten and was in the hospital with collapsed lungs, my dad's shotgun and rifle were in police evidence and our home had been searched and destroyed. We set about putting it back together. One of the most impactful parts of my 8th-grade year was meeting people from around the world- everyone wasn't white or black, they were Russian, Indian, Puerto Rican, Mexican, Irish, English, European, Polish, so many other things, who knew the world was so big. 8th grade, New Jersey changed my life, and in the Summer I graduated 8th grade and I was set to start my freshman year of High School- we were moving back to Alabama but this time we weren't going to live in Wilmer- they were hoping to remove my brother from the influence of Meth, weed, cocaine, and alcohol so we moved closer to the beach.

High school

Summer of 2002, moving back to Alabama from New Jersey was an adventure, I was approaching the age of 15, I had this unique opportunity to reinvent myself, I was finally becoming a woman, and I was ready to start high school. I was an Aunt, I was at a crucial point in my life, and I was so nervous. My eyes were open to the fact that the world was not so simple, it was filled with pain, confusion, anger, loss, drugs, alcohol, people that would hurt you. I started high school friendless and nervous, I remember choosing my classes, I hated PE so I wanted to avoid it, but couldn't. I wanted to be a Marine biologist do biology classes and math were a must, I loved History so history was a must. I found my group soon, a group of kids who like me just wanted to focus on school, who went to school early to spend time in the library reading books, who took an interest in playing chess and who it turns out were in Marching Band. I made an appointment with the band director and asked if I could join the band as a shadow marcher since I was late in joining and he let me. I made friends- we spent hours practicing our music, practicing choreography for marching-as a shadow marcher I had to memorize different positions to be able to fill in for anyone absent from a football game or performance, as a band member I got to participate in marching in parades, be part of the football games, and develop friendships. Marching band became my life when we were not doing band my friends and I were talking about movies, making plans to hang out on the weekends and just studying for school. One of my friends had gotten held back a year so she was the first of us to turn 16 years old, we were so excited because now we didn't have to rely on our parents to drive us around, we made plans to go to the movies. That Summer before band camp began we began the tradition of going to the movies and Chinese food, boys weren't even on our minds, our focus was band, music, Lord of the Rings, and Chinese food. It was one of the best summers of my life in High School. End of Summer brought along Band Camp, I was no longer a shadow marcher, we were given our spots, for the upcoming choreography, we spent 8 hours a day during Summer practicing music, marches, doing push-ups when we didn't stand at attention fast enough, and we were getting pumped for football season aka marching band season, also for the fact that we would be traveling as a band to Walt Disney World without parents. It was going to be an exciting year.

10th grade began with the annual beginning of school pep rally bonfire, as a member of the marching band we were there early to get the crowd engaged and excited as the football players and cheerleaders came out to continue the excitement, soon after the bonfire we had our first football game of the year- the first game was always the most exciting, our first chance to show off our skills, to ride the band bus, and to just have fun. It was a muddy experience as it decided to rain but not enough to keep us from marching so away we went marching in the mud, rolling our feet, keeping to the beat, playing our instruments, cheering on the football team, after the game riding back on the bus filled with excitement. That year one of my friends began dating a senior and would tell us about her adventures, they were interesting but not enough to want to join in the dating game. Lord of the Rings and the adventures of Monty Python held all of my interest. Also, I was approaching Winter when I would be traveling to Germany with my parents and after that, I would be starting driver's ed and finally be able to drive myself. Going to Germany was one of the coolest experiences I had ever done, here I was a 15 year old and I was going to Germany- a small village called Rendsburg, my dad was there working on the owner of Victoria's Secret Yacht, we arrived via a flight from Paris and was introduced to what really cold weather was like, what community was like, and we were welcomed into the Inn like we were family. I was used to people being friendly but this was a whole new level of friendliness. They were offering us weird food, drinks, and acting as if we were family instead of merely being hotel guests. My parents permitted me to wander around as I wanted, I was 15 and it was acceptable to walk to the village to go shopping, try new foods, talk with people. I was excited, most people could speak some English, and those who couldn't we could communicate in a variety of misspoken German and misspoken English, it was amazing. Everything was so festive, they took the meaning of Christmas very seriously, everywhere were Christmas trees and decorations, mulled wine, and little chocolate figurines. Christmas came about and it was a quiet affair we went to Chinese food where everyone got this German wine shot including me and we sipped it in cheers (I passed mine to my dad as soon as I tasted it) and after dinner, we went back to our Inn where my parents slept off their wine. After Christmas the village began preparing for the New Years celebration of roasting a pig, and my mom and I traveled to Hamburg to explore, traveled to Munich to see some Ice Sculptures, and finally went to Berlin where I got to explore what I was most curious about- the Berlin Wall and the history of World War 2, I took many notes to turn into my history teacher once I was back home to get extra credit. We left Germany to head back to Alabama a few days before the New year.

Once back home, my friends and I began our weekly movie and Chinese nights, I got serious about driving and began my driving education class, and in March I passed my driving exam and got my license and simultaneously got a car for my birthday. My parents always spoiled me which was nice but also hard because my brother Chris only hated me, putting me down often whenever he wasn't busy stealing things from stores with his girlfriend. I began my first real job as a sales associate and my evenings and weekends got busy when I wasn't working, doing marching band, I would drive to the beach with my friends, go to the movies, Chinese food, and hang out. Disney world was coming up and my mom and I went shopping for a new wardrobe, I was excited.

The day we boarded the bus to Disney world was uneventful, my friend Amy and I would be sitting together for the 8-hour trip, and she, I, and our friend Heather would be rooming together. Here's one thing they never tell you about long trips, girls aren't meant to room together for a week- it's stressful and puts friendship to a true test. Somehow we survived it with only one argument, we spent the week riding rides, going on roller coasters, laughing, giggling, exploring, and ending the week by marching in the Disney world parade, we traveled home exhausted but happy.

Once back from Disney World life continued, the high school continued, work was going well, hanging out with my friends was going well, we would spend our weekends, our free time hanging out, watching movies, making silly videos, and eating lots of Chinese food and Mexican food. Summer was approaching, my dad was considering a position at a new company in Washington state and I was excited to spend the summer working, saving money, and going to the beach with friends. Summer came, I was working during the day, one summer day I met an older guy and we began a flirtation, it was fun, exciting, but it was meaningless- he was my first kiss, he smelled like cigarettes and it was the worst experience of that summer. At the end of June, my parents and I flew to Florida to go on a cruise ship that would take us to the Virgin Islands and the Bahamas, I was excited to have a vacation. Onboard the ship I soon met kids my age and we began hanging out every day and night going to the teen club, dancing hours away, and wandering the ship all night long often falling asleep on lounge chairs after spending all night talking or hitting the buffet. It was fun, it was a sense of freedom, a sense of camaraderie. That week on the cruise ship was a fun experience- seeing the

Bahamas, the Virgin Islands, dancing, exploring, making friends, and soon after deboarding and going back to real life.

A few weeks after returning from the cruise trip my brother Chris was arrested and sentenced to time in a juvenile prison facility, and my mom and I flew to Washington state to look for a home to rent for our upcoming relocation. We had a week and my mom and I took to looking all over the Puget Sound area, we eventually found a place in Federal Way, Washington and secured it by signing a lease, we flew back to Alabama with the knowledge that by the end of July we would be relocating across the country- again, this time we would be settling permanently in the Pacific Northwest. I was nervous, I was excited, I was apprehensive, I was leaving behind my friends, my brother was being left behind in prison, but my dad had a great opportunity, so we loaded up the dogs, we loaded up our belongings, my car, and away we went driving from Alabama to Washington state. It was a miserably long trip, driving hour after hour with my parents, them bickering at almost every stop we made, the Uhaul breaking down, in Kansas my car lost one of its fenders, I was upset, everything was going horrible, I was being transplanted halfway through high school, I was losing my friends, my life was over.

Eventually, we made it to Washington state, my Aunt and Uncle had driven three hours to help us unpack our Uhaul, it was a momentous day, here we were settling into our new house, settling in, finally getting the chance to drive my car again. The first weeks in Washington were busy, we had to request transcripts from my school in Alabama, register my car, pass my driver's licensing test, and get settled in. A few things happened those first few days, Washington state wouldn't accept a license from the state of Alabama due to me being only 16 at the time, and Alabama not having Sarah, roundabouts, or other odd driving restrictions, but I was not going to give up-no way was this state going to take away my ability to drive my car. So I wrote to the Alabama state legislator pleading with them to write me a letter granting my license to be accepted in Washington state and miraculously that accepted it, I got my transcripts and got enrolled into eleventh grade in the local high school, and I began looking for a new job. Life settled into a schedule, I got a job working at a local fast-food restaurant, I started going to school, I began making friends-eventually.

Making friends in Washington state was not easy- people, kids, were so different, they were harder, more closed off, so much more "advanced" they were having sex, flirting, staying out all hours of the night, I had kissed one guy, I hadn't had a boyfriend before, I didn't stay out all night, and I wanted to join the band. I quickly realized that I wanted to fit in more than I wanted anything else, I was tired of being fat, I was tired of being the geek smart girl. I wanted friends, I wanted to be liked, I didn't want to be pointed at, I didn't want to be known as the girl with the sweet southern accent, lowered eclipse, and slightly overweight. I didn't want to join the band, I registered for PE aerobics class, I braved the locker room, I stopped eating so much and started throwing up when I did eat, I made friends, I took people for rides in my car, and I continued chatting all hours of the night with random strangers on the internet who understood me.

Chat rooms looking back was my first addiction-before I started throwing up before I realized my love of food as a coping mechanism, I loved the ability to slip on different personas, to be someone different, stronger, sexier, more fun. I could do that in chat rooms, I could be a dominant woman and boss around submissive men, I loved spending hours role-playing BDSM games in chat rooms until I met a new friend who would introduce me to real-life chat rooms, rooms where I would meet and chat with my first boyfriend. Chatting with real-life guys around the Seattle area was a whole new experience my friend and I would race home from school and go to her house where her mom was never home, she would pop open a can of beer and hand me a soda and we would browse the chat rooms looking for potential guys to talk to. Eventually we found a few such guys, we would begin chatting laughing and giggling at how lame they were, sending fake photos of faces of actresses we found online, and then one day we decided to take it a step further, we were both going to meet two guys we had been talking with for weeks. We were scared and nervous but we arranged for me to sleepover at her house, we would go to the local teenage club to dance and meet up with them there.

The night we were to meet up with the guys we set about getting ready- I didn't have anything to wear, my wardrobe was still all about my old persona of Southern girl band greek, so my friend helped me, we dressed in short skirts and shorts, we applied makeup, put high heels on, got in my car and drove away to the club. On the way to the club we ended hitting a snag when exiting an offramp of the freeway- I got rear-ended by a woman who had been driving to fast and had had too much to drink. After a time the cops came and gave both the woman and me tickets, I had stopped too suddenly, and she had been driving too fast. After receiving the ticket and ascertaining the car was able to be driven we continued to the club. We arrived at the club and spent the night dancing, we eventually met up with the guys which both of them turned out to be nice, we danced, we laughed, and I went home alone leaving behind my friend who had chosen to continue hanging out with the guy she had met.

The next day the guy and I started texting each other, slowly getting to know each other through texts and phone calls, chatting online. We made plans to hang out in a few weeks and go to the movies and out to dinner. I was going to have my first date with a guy, sure he was 9 years older than I was, but I was excited, nervous, and looking forward to it. The date went well movies, dinner, and talking, and I went home and worked on French homework. I fell into a routine chatting with my new boyfriend, working, and doing homework. My grades were dropping just like my weight, I was getting skinnier, and life was on the upswing of excitement. I invited my boyfriend to Thanksgiving dinner that year to meet my parents who still didn't know about the age difference between us, it was going to be an exciting moment.

Thanksgiving came- my boyfriend came to dinner and would soon after be known as the deviled egg guy cause he wouldn't stop talking about them, maybe he was nervous but it was embarrassing, my brother came as well-he had been released from prison and had arrived in Washington state rougher, meaner, and happy to be eating real food. Thanksgiving was relatively uneventful we spent the day eating so that by the time the turkey was cooked we were not hungry, we scoured advertisements to find the best places to go black Friday shopping and eventually we ate dinner, ate the pie, and counted down till 4 am when we could begin shopping. Black Friday shopping was a ritual my family and I had for many years- we fell into the American trap of commercialism- at first as a kid it was a way for my parents to afford Christmas presents- later it was just they got sucked into it- it was an endorphin rush, a high similar to smoking, drinking, or using drugs.

Christmas was approaching it was going to be a fun experience, I was working more hours, I had made new friends and was spending my free time hanging out with my new friends, growing tired of going to school, spending my free time with my boyfriend, and occasionally fitting in time for school work. The school had lost its appeal, I was struggling, struggling with kids making fun of me, of my accent, struggling with my weight which I was steadily losing, struggling with life in high school. Christmas came the boyfriend drove us down to Portland for a day to hang out and explore his hometown, a few weeks previously he had created a magical moment and I had officially become a woman, but I was struggling too with that, why had I chosen this guy, but I just kept convincing myself it was no big deal. Soon I was going to be 17, life would be changing, and the boyfriend was making talks of us going to Singapore together as a birthday present to me. I began talking to my parents after the first of the year about the possibility of me going to Singapore. My dad was not happy-no way was his 16-year-old girl going to Singapore with a 26-year-old. But I just kept asking, asking my dad and my mom, finally I convinced them to let me go-go with my mom as a chaperone.

The trip was in early March, my mom and I boarded a plane to go to Singapore, we had plans of things to visit, things to do while there, mainly shopping. We arrived in Singapore and began exploring the night markets, the different neighborhoods, the beach, zoo, and eventually the boyfriend arrived. We made plans to visit each other when he got leave from his duty that had brought him to Singapore, the night we met up included mass amounts of vodka and my first experience of getting wasted. I just kept drinking glass after glass of vodka- I couldn't taste it, I didn't feel it so surely it wasn't working, until one glass too many led to me throwing up, embarrassing myself, crying, and getting angry at the boyfriend. I hated this feeling. I hated being drunk, I felt out of control, I couldn't stand up, I couldn't move, I constantly had to pee, my stomach hurt, my head hurt, I kept throwing up. What was this horrible feeling, and why was this person seeing me so vulnerable. I hated it, I hated the feeling of being drunk, of being out of control, soon enough he managed to get me back to my mom's hotel room where she had been waiting for me. She was not happy-she could smell alcohol on me, but she said nothing until the next morning when she opened the curtains and informed me we were going to spend the day outside exploring. My first hangover experience was not fun- headache, dehydration, throbbing body, nausea, and the sun was so bright, how did people do this? How was I going to survive this agony- food helped, though the first amount of food soon after left my body, but eventually I began feeling better, the more water I drank the better I felt, I swore to myself that day I would not drink like that again, I never wanted this experience again.

Coming back from Singapore I was a changed person, I was different, I wasn't so naive, I had opened my eyes to so many things- the first of which was that I was going to dump my boyfriend. He was old, he took advantage of me, he saw me at a disadvantage, and no one was allowed to see me at such a vulnerable state. The next thing I knew was that I was tired of high school- it wasn't working for me, I was sick of the kids, tired of molding myself to other people's standards, and I was sick of being treated like a kid. I wasn't a kid, I had a car, I had a job, I could work full time and get a place of my own. As soon as I got back from Singapore I told my parents my plans, I was quitting high school, I was going to work full time, and I was no longer going to live with them. I had just turned 17 and I was on top of the world. My dad, however, did not agree with me-he was so angry, it was the first time I had ever disappointed him, he was livid, we got into a major argument that resulted in him trying to hit me with a belt as if I was still a kid. Looking back I know he was just frustrated but him attempting to hit me only made my plan more important. I ran away from home that night-bruised, angry, hurt, and went to a coworker's apartment. I told her what had happened, she was my age but had been emancipated and was considered an adult, I asked her if she would want to get a place together- she agreed and we began searching for apartments to live in.

Late Teens

Two weeks later, I packed up my belongings while my dad was out of town, I said bye to my mom and I moved into my new room in a three-bedroom apartment I was going to share with two other girls. It wasn't ideal but I was so excited to have the freedom to come and go as I please. We settled into a routine of working, hanging out, and relaxing at home. Eventually, we started planning our first party, one of the roommates wanted to throw a party-an excuse to drink, to talk to guys, to have fun, I was nervous I wasn't into drinking the way she was, and guys-guys were unnecessary I was enjoying being single. The night of the party we each drank a wine cooler, and got our place ready, people arrived and started drinking heavily, smoking weed, cigarettes, within an hour I had locked myself in my room- I hated that they were drunk, I hated the smoke, the people, some people knocked on my door but I ignored them. I was tired, I was still making myself throw up throughout the day and the one wine cooler made me tired- I eventually fell asleep and woke up the next morning to people passed out everywhere, a disastrous house, and the sick feeling that I was never going to be safe here. I started looking for someone to take over my room so I could move out. I hated living with them-they wanted to drink and party, to hookup with guys, I wanted to smile, to dance, to watch movies, and to make money. I just didn't want to be bothered by my parents but parents were better than this.

I moved back in with my parents and for the first time in my life, I got depressed. I wasn't eating, I wasn't drinking water, I couldn't sleep- I just stayed in my room for hours only emerging when it was time to go to work. I could barely lift my arms, I was unhappy and miserable, I was skinny, and yet I felt out of control. I was disappointed in myself, in my choices but I couldn't tell anyone that. Eventually my mom forced me to the doctor, she told the doctor about me and the doctor prescribed me depression medicine and sleeping tablets, once home my mom gave me the medicine and told me to take a bath- I did as I was told I was too weak to do anything else, inside the bathtub I fell asleep, luckily my mom came to check on me soon after I had fallen asleep- the sleeping tablet depression medicine combination had knocked me out, she carried me to my bed, dressed me, and I slept for what felt like days. I woke up and ate and finally felt more energized though slightly sick from the food. My mom was on a mission to make me eat, the doctor had informed her my body weight, my body mass index was too little for my body- I was underweight, I didn't have enough body fat, I was 115 pounds, 5 feet 5.5 inches, and my BMI was around 16.5, my mom was worried, she was also worried about my attitude to it. She had a lot to worry about between an underweight bulimic daughter to a meth-addicted son who had knocked up his girlfriend she was overwhelmed.

Eventually, I began eating, I gained a few pounds and my mom lost interest in making me eat. I was gaining strength feeling back to normal mentally and physically and I began making plans to move out, I was planning to move into my first apartment as soon as I turned 18 I was going to move in my best friend David the only problem was that he wasn't a US citizen and while he had forged documents to get work but the apartment wouldn't accept them, without his income I didn't qualify alone for 3 times the income so I decided to ask a boyfriend if he would want to move into an apartment with me we made plans to live together.

Moving in with two guys was a new adventure, my parents helped me to move into the apartment and wished me the best of luck, the boyfriend moved in his stuff, and our friend soon joined us. It wasn't an ideal living experience but it was a fun living experience. Every night was a party, if you considered watching guys smoke weed, eat food, laugh at cartoons a party, and every morning was a disaster of dirty dishes and clothes strewn everywhere. I was miserable but I couldn't complain instead I did the best I could, I would attempt to clean up but it soon became a resentful job, as the woman is the one in charge of cooking, cleaning, and working full time was too much. I was upset, I lost all desire for the boyfriend who was becoming more adventurous in the bedroom sex antics spending hours watching porn while stoned out of his mind, asking to experiment with things that made me uncomfortable. It was my first test at boundaries and I was failing. I wanted to make him happy, I wanted to please everyone, and I was suffering as a result. I started smoking weed, it was an outlet, a way to fall asleep. I hated the effect, I hated smoking weed, getting sleepy, eating peanut butter so as soon as I tried it I realized it wasn't for me.

A year passed as roommates, I was no longer interested in maintaining a relationship with a boyfriend but I felt stuck, I wanted my friend to have a place to live, so we began to approach the topic of getting a larger place, my friend knew I was not happy with my boyfriend and was contemplating dumping him. My boyfriend was oblivious and pushing new things in sex such as toys, strap-ons, porn, and other things that I was getting frustrated with. I had no desire for him and spent hours creating excuse after excuse not to be alone with him, not to have sex, I would sleep on the couch to avoid him. I suspected him of being gay but I didn't want to confront him as it wasn't my place. I found out in June of 2007, my parents and I were going to be going to Hawaii to take a cruise and the boyfriend was coming with us- I was dreading it so I made the rash decision to dump him a week before we were due to depart for Hawaii. The relationship was over, I was tired of our messy house, tired of being the sole cooker, tired of living like a slob and being expected to be the maid. I was tired of him. I was tired of parties, and guys coming over to our house and making fun of us and then getting high.

The day I broke up with my boyfriend he acted like the world was ending, I couldn't comprehend what the big deal was. Later I realized he was sad, he was losing his mother replacement and would be moving back in with his mom. He thought he loved me. It was a convenience, but I was done with being a convenience. He went out with his friends the night we broke up and I went out with my best friend who was also our roommate. He chose to go to strip clubs where one of his friends spent the evening sending me texts and flirting with me. My friend and I went to a salsa party, took E, and drank beer. We got wasted and spent the night dancing, laughing, and listening to heartbreak songs. When I got so wasted that I blacked out in the bathroom he was the one who came and found me before the other guys at the party found me, he is the one who held my hair back when I began throwing up, and he is the one he drove us home until he fell asleep at the steering wheel. Somehow- fate, a higher power, luck I woke up and woke him up and we didn't hit a freeway concrete divider and we made it home in one piece. We passed out on the couch and woke up the next morning to have a late breakfast together. He was my best friend and he supported me during a breakup. We discussed him and the ex-boyfriend sharing a room, I would have my room back to myself, and we would finish out our lease which had only a few short months left on it.

The ex-boyfriend's friend and I hung out together the day after he had taken my ex to the strip club, we went to his friend's party and spent the night laughing and drinking. He was funny, he was young, and he had an amazing car. After the party, after drinking for hours, after getting cornered in the party by his friend and another guy and becoming hysterical after they attempted to take advantage of me we left and went home. Drunk driving was a thing back then, and he would take us on a windy road and drive fast while under the influence. It was reckless, it was stupid, it was exhilarating. We slept together that night, it was a lust-filled drunken night together and I soon realized I had thrown up my birth control pills and I couldn't remember if we had used protection or if he had pulled out, the next morning was a panic-filled morning of getting to a Planned Parenthood clinic and taking the morning-after pill. As soon as I took the pill I made a promise to myself to never find myself in the same situation, if this is what alcohol was going to do to me I didn't want to drink, not to mention my head felt horrible.

The week passed in a blur of romantic moments, decreased drinking, and scrambling to pack my suitcase to head to Hawaii. Hawaii was going to be amazing even if my ex was coming, I was looking forward to sunbathing, surfing, exploring, and eating amazing food. The flight to Hawaii was uneventful, arriving on the Big Island of Hawaii was a magical sight to be seen, and boarding the cruise was a simple matter, the awkwardness of where my ex was to sleep began shortly after- he was hoping the cruise would rekindle our relationship and I was dreading sleeping. We reached an unspoken agreement to hang out but there would be no sex, he would stop pressuring me or I would lock him out of the room, and we would spend the

7-day cruise having fun. The first day of the cruise was spent at sea which meant I spent the day on the top level of the cruise ship laying in the sun, I had forgotten my Carribean cruise and the sunburn I received back in 2004. At the end of the first day as I was taking a shower I realized I was sunburnt-not only was I sunburnt I was in agony. My skin was red, it was hurting, I couldn't bear to have clothes on, lotion didn't help, and the shower was pure torture. I had forgotten to put sunscreen on, but I wasn't going to let a sunburn derail my entire trip. I soaked in black tea, I applied aloe vera, I put mass quantities of coconut oil on my skin, took Tylenol, and continued with my trip.

Windsurfing, hiking, shopping, exploring, and trips to the ocean were the most amazing experiences to be had during the day. Hawaii was a beautiful place and the islands were each unique. The days were spent having fun and wincing in pain of the sunburn, the evenings were spent avoiding the ex-boyfriend who spent the evenings crying and begging me to rub him with oil. He taught me a lot that week-how to say no, how to walk away, how to never put myself in a similar position. He taught me what I didn't want. I counted down the days until I would return to Washington and back to my life. I missed working, I was looking forward to returning to my position as a perfume sales manager. The day we flew back I told my ex I didn't think I could continue sharing a place with him-I didn't want to wake up in the middle of the night to him trying to pick my lock or get into my bedroom, our relationship was over and he needed to move on. I wasn't interested and I didn't want to lead him on. I was hanging out with his friend and I had met someone else who I was planning to hang out once back home.

We got off the plane and started our drive home, we hadn't heard from our other roommate all week and were wondering what he was up to. As soon as we reached our apartment we knew something was wrong. There were holes in our windows, our door was open and had police tape on the front of it. We had received a letter from our apartment telling us we were expected to fix the windows as soon as possible and that the swat team had broken into our apartment and arrested an unregistered tenant-we had violated our lease and our lease was not going to be renewed, we could stay until the end of it only because there were only 60 days left. It took a few days to piece together what had happened while we were in Hawaii. Our roommate had been dating a girl who had a boyfriend, he was in love with her and she had called him in the middle of the night hysterical, he was kind, loyal, loving guy and he rode to her rescue with a friend, together him and the friend rescued the girl, in the midst of rescuing the girl our friend had shot the girl's boyfriend and killed him. He fled the scene with his friend and the girl and they had hidden out in our apartment till the next day when the reality of what had happened hit the girl and she left, his friend also left to his own home and our friend stayed behind watching the news realizing someone had seen him and the cops were searching for him. Eventually, the cops traced the evidence and/or got a confession from the girl confirming our friend as the shooter, our friend took the blame never mentioning the accomplice to the crime, he never told anyone to this day who was with him at the shooting. I went to visit him in jail during his arraignment, trial, and sentencing, he got 20 years in prison, reduced to 12-15 for good behavior for first degree murder, he wasn't a US citizen and was in the country illegally with forged documents and would be deported after serving his time back to Mexico. I moved out of the apartment and left my ex there to live alone, he had found a roommate to replace me, and I happily moved on with my life. I was going to move in with his friend, we were in lust and enjoying each other, he was ready to move out of his parent's house and we decided to move in with his friends who had just bought a house. It was convenient to my work, and it kept me from having to live with my parents again.

I moved out of the apartment and in with my new guy, we weren't planning a future but we were having fun. It wasn't the greatest sex but it was fun. We spent the weekend drinking and driving, smoking weed. August and September passed in a blur and at some point, I decided to switch jobs and go back to working with children. It was a bittersweet choice, on the one hand, I love being a teacher but on the other, I was going to miss being in charge of a store, but I had made my decision and decided to follow through, the day I quit I spent the night getting drunk with the guy. The next day I was to begin as a preschool teacher to 3 and 4-year-olds I was excited at the prospect of going back to teaching.

Going back to being a full-time teacher was an adjustment, I would work the typical 9-6 spending my day bossing around small children with large opinions on what they wanted to do, come home and spend the evening eating, drinking, and or getting high, falling asleep late into the night. It became a trend

Monday to Friday falling into this new pattern and preparing for the weekend which would mean attending a party. I lost track of days but by the end of September I was starting to feel off, I had just finished attending a state training to be fully certified as a preschool teacher and one of the women jokingly mentioned the word pregnant. The saying of pregnancy being in the water was thrown aloud but I just laughed it off, I was 19, I was on the pill, the few blunders had been followed by taking a morning-after pill, sure I spent the weekends drinking and sometimes throwing up but there was no way I could be pregnant. I chalked it up to working too many hours and continued on with my life, going to work, coming home, I made a goal to go to bed earlier, I started drinking more energy drinks, and forgot about the silly joke.

Knocked Up Let's Get Married

The beginning of October 2007 rolled around and the Autumn festivities for the preschool kicked off in full force, Autumn was one of the most exciting times as a teacher it meant lesson plans filled with apple tasting and pumpkin carving, that would lead to Thanksgiving, and Winter Holidays. I was excited but still unmotivated, something was wrong with me, I was always tired, I lost my appetite, I couldn't eat without feeling nauseous, and the caffeine wasn't working. I had slowed down on my drinking, only drinking on the weekends and not as much as I had been. I made the decision to make an annual exam with my doctor, I was nervous but I went to the doctors office and told her honestly what was going on- she suggested a pregnancy test- I told her I had taken a few of them from over the counter and all showed negative so she ordered a blood pregnancy test, and a variety of other tests and assured me I would know about the pregnancy start everything else was fine. I went home that day full of dread and went to work later in the afternoon, around 5 pm as I was doing the evening cleaning for the classroom, my life changed forever. The doctor called me excitedly- I was pregnant, she said since I wasn't showing on the over the counter tests that I wasn't probably very far along and I have options. I was numb, I was devastated, I was scared, I couldn't tell anyone so I made an appointment with the referred Obstetrician to find out how far along I was, finished my workday and went home to figure out how to tell the guy I was pregnant.

At home that night I had asked the guy to come home earlier than his norm so that we could talk, I have no idea what he was thinking- I was nervous, I wanted a drink but I was pregnant and couldn't risk alcohol causing harm to my baby. I had already begun thinking about it as my baby, this small blip inside me was a forming human-the idea of causing it harm was inconceivable. The guy arrived home, I took a breath, I was scared, I was trembling, I told him I was knocked up-I didn't know how it had happened, I was on birth control, but it had happened. I hadn't decided yet what I was going to do, but I didn't believe in abortion, to me, abortion was harming an innocent, sure he could have an opinion but it was my body and ultimately I would weigh his opinion but I couldn't harm a child. He was in shock I don't think he really knew what to say or what to do, I had thrown a variety of bombs on him, I wouldn't have an abortion and I was pregnant, he was 21 and I was going to ruin his life. We went to bed that night not really talking or addressing the fact of the pregnancy, I was giving him time to process and to talk to his friends, what I didn't know at the time was that his friends were advising him to push me for abortion, they were filling his head with ideas, lies, thoughts. They were telling him that I was a slut, I was after his money, I had gotten pregnant on purpose, that I had slept around. When he confronted me I was sad, we had a connection, I thought he believed me, but friends versus a girl he was sleeping with had lost their value of importance, I was now the evil chick who got knocked up, it was my fault and in his mind there was no going back from that.

I was depressed, I was lost at what to do, I talked with some coworkers, I talked to my mom and confessed to her what was going on. She was so angry, she didn't like the guy and had multiple times confronted us and him, she didn't want me to be with him, she certainly didn't want me to have his baby but she knew how I felt about abortion because it was a belief shared with her and my father. She asked me what I had planned to do, I told her I was confused and uncertain about what to do, I couldn't have an abortion. My mom invited my guy and me to attend her birthday dinner on the 11th of October and in the meantime, I needed to come to a decision on what I was going to do, I was young, I had my entire future ahead of me, I had just been promoted to a higher position as a teacher, I had to choose what I wanted and needed in my life.

Life with the guy had gotten difficult he was smoking more weed, he was miserable, his friends were whispering in his ear and he was sending me hurtful emails, he was scared just like I was. He knew I was reaching a decision and he wasn't going to like it-he knew I wasn't willing to have an abortion. The day I made my decision I dragged him with me to dinner with my parents, at dinner it was a very awkward experience my dad was furious, he hated the guy, he eyed him with distaste, and he asked him what his intentions were for his daughter. My dad refused to talk to me until he figured out the guy, my dad's only concern was for me. He wanted to protect me and he didn't trust the guy, my dad had already spoken with me, he told me I should move home, live with my parents, let them help me raise the baby, don't get stuck with the guy. I had a crazy idea fueled by my mom that I should get married. It was a stupid idea, but I latched onto it, he had knocked me up, that's what people do when they get pregnant, they get married. I told my dad at the dinner I was going to marry the guy, the guy agreed, and we went home with the decision that was going to forever change our lives.

October 25 was the day we decided to get married, he requested the day off of work as did I, I went and bought a wedding dress-I knew that this was going to be my only opportunity to wear one, there would be no fairy tale wedding for me, so at least I wanted to feel like a princess even if it was for a shotgun wedding. I got the dress, I got shoes, flowers, a tiara, I booked the time slot with the judge, filed the forms to be married, and submitted payment. It was happening, I was to be married at the age of 19, I was knocked up and would be a mom before I could legally drink alcohol. I was terrified, was I making the right choice? Was I going to regret this? The guy was scared. We set a time before the wedding to meet with his parents to tell them the news of my pregnancy and our upcoming marriage.

The day we went for dinner at his parents was a day like any other day, I had never met them before, they were Russian, they spoke some English and like any other girl, I was worried about if they would like me. What they were going to think of me? Dinner was an interesting experience of new foods that smelled bad, and stilted conversation. They didn't know why their son was bringing a girl home, but they were polite to me. Halfway through the dinner, we told them I was pregnant, or rather the guy told them in Russian about me being pregnant, they looked at me, and launched into conversation with him ignoring me, he told them about us getting married and once again a loud rambunctious Russian conversation ensued. By the end of the dinner which I spent eating and trying not to throw up the conversation wound down to a normal level of talk and his parents told me they would come to our wedding and to send them the details, his mom was both excited and unhappy about becoming a grandmother. His parents put on their fake smiles for me, but inside the guy and I both knew they weren't happy. His parents, his grandma, his friends, his family, everyone in his life was telling him to make me have an abortion, I was the only person telling him I wouldn't. I was the one forcing him to marry me. He was miserable, but he knew I wasn't going to change my mind. October 25, 2007, came, the morning of our wedding our roommates texted him demanding he take out the garbage, I was furious, I was nauseous with morning sickness, and I reacted negatively to her, we got ready and left for the courthouse, my dad was in Korea, but my brother, his baby, wife, and my mom were going to come and be witnesses for me, my guy's parents were coming to be witnesses for him. Once we arrived at the courthouse my family was there ready and waiting to support me in the wedding adventure, my guy's parents were nowhere to be seen, he tried calling them but they didn't answer their phones, so we went up to the Judge's courtroom and our wedding began. My brother's wife would be a witness for my guy, the wedding was over fast a simple exchange of words, the guy's face was a priceless moment, looking back at the pictures of him I just have to laugh, he was miserable, angry, and he didn't want to be there but he says I forced him so he did it anyway. After getting married we went for breakfast as Igor and wife and spent the day doing what would have been done any other day, talking, engaging each other in conversation and by the end of the day I was exhausted from trying to feign happiness.

A few days later we went to Seattle for a mini-honeymoon, we were going to pretend happiness and excitement at being married. We celebrated at a fancy restaurant where we lackluster dipped food into cheese, broth, and chocolate, and went back to our hotel to celebrate in privacy. It wasn't a magical fairy tale wedding, it was a strained event of us both doing what we had to do. We had made our choices and we were sticking to them. After the weekend of our honeymoon we went back into our routine of working, I was struggling, I couldn't stop throwing up, I was only craving chocolate but the chocolate was betraying me, I could barely drive, I couldn't stomach food, water was a chore. Morning sickness hit at all hours of the day, especially in the evenings when people were cooking, I was desperate to not feel like throwing up, the guy was smoking weed nonstop constantly in a bubble of weed bliss. I was angry and desperate and asked him one day to let me try weed to help with nausea, there were mixed reports about the effects it has on a fetus, I took a puff, felt better, ate, and fell asleep. The next morning I regretted it, what if I had hurt the baby? I vowed to never again do weed and steeled myself to deal with nausea. By mid-November pregnancy was on its way, I had visited and had my first ultrasound to determine when the baby would be born accompanied by the new Igor and his mother-a grueling experience of having my privacy invaded. The doctor happened to be Russian and she and the doctor spent the entire visit discussing my pregnancy without consulting me. I was angry and I vowed never again to return to the doctor nor would I ever allow her to come to an appointment with me. I did find out I was over 11 weeks pregnant and I would be due sometime in June 2008. After the appointment, we discussed moving to our own place and hosting a housewarming party. A few days later we had found a house and prepared to move in, our housewarming party was set for a week before Thanksgiving, and we started buying furniture, accepted furniture for our new place. The place just happened to be a few short blocks away from his friends which allowed him to continue partying with them easily and have an escape away from his pregnant wife.

The housewarming party was a new experience, I had only invited my parents and brother's family, my Igor invited his parents and his parents invited all of their friends. People began showing up with a bottle after a bottle of vodka, borscht, and other Russian foods were served. People talked louder and louder often yelling at each other especially as they drank more and more vodka. This party was loud, it was intimidating and I spent most of it silent, my parents and family left quickly, they were not impressed with the drinking, and they didn't want to be a part of it. The Russians spent the evening drinking, laughing, discussing things, convincing my new Igor of his status in life. After the party as I was being hugged by many Russians, my in-laws made plans to come for dinner soon so that my mother in law could show me how to cook some Russian dishes and we could discuss furnishings and baby items. I agreed and away they went.

Thanksgiving was approaching, I was excited I loved the holidays and Thanksgiving was the start of it. Thanksgiving also meant black Friday shopping and I was going to continue the tradition of going with my parents to shop-this year would mean buying baby stuff. We went for Thanksgiving dinner at my parents' home and invited my ex to go with us as he had no one else to spend it with. We had remained friends and it proved to be an interesting experience. My brother it seemed had stolen my ex's tires, a fancy set of wheels for his car and wouldn't give them back to my ex, my brother didn't like my Igor and he liked my ex even less. The ex had brought his mother with him, and so this strange gathering was formed ending with my ex accusing my brother, my brother trying to fight my ex, the ex's mom accusing my family of stealing her purse (she later realized she had left it in her car) and my father demanding the ex to leave the house. I was miserable. I was exhausted and I was delighted to go shopping and forget the dreadful experience. My Igor went home, my brother, mom, dad, and I loaded up and went Black Friday shopping.

After the Thanksgiving experience my ex apologized to my family and to me, my brother refused to give up the wheels saying my ex deserved it and life continued on. I began writing to my old friend who was in prison, and my Igor continued working. Things settled into a routine, I was working the Igor was working and life moved on. My Igor and I weren't talking and the resentments grew. Shortly before Christmas, my Igor told me I had ruined his life, he hated me, and he couldn't believe he fell into my trap. I had trapped him, gotten a rich Igor, and gotten knocked up on purpose. I was angry, hurt, and upset and I left him- I went to my parent's house who immediately suggested separation they still weren't fans of his, they knew he spent every evening getting high and drunk with his friends, they saw me depressed and miserable, they knew I was unhappy. They wanted to help me, but I had put myself in this position. I was miserable because I deserve to be miserable, I was unhappy because I did this, I was going to be a mom, and the kids deserve a dad. I tried talking to the Igor and eventually, we found a sort of peace together.

Christmas arrived and I was excited to spend it with my family, my niece was coming and I was so happy to see her opening presents, though of course, she was only 3 months old, my Igor was going to attend Christmas with my family since he was Russian and their primary Christmas falls on New Year's eve and on January 7 it worked out well. Christmas day was just like any other family Christmas waking up at 5 am, counting down till it was time to wake my parents, me making my dad his signature cappuccino with the perfect foam and asking them if we could open presents, my dad jokingly demanding breakfast first, and bribing him withholding his granddaughter. By 8 am presents were opened, and the food was being made, the other brothers and their families would arrive around noon. It was a nice Christmas, the first as a married woman. My Igor sat there quiet much of the day, drinking beer as soon as it was offered to him. By afternoon the house was filled with kids and adults some drinking and some not, bellies filled and laughs to be heard. We excuse ourselves early to go to his parent's house for dinner where we had dinner and I sat there quietly. Thankfully my morning sickness had passed but my stomach still didn't accept Russian food well.

After Christmas we began preparing for the New Year, what would we do, where would we go, who we spend it with. It didn't matter to me, New Year's Eve had never really been my thing and it would be even less important to me this year since I was pregnant. In the end, we decided we would spend NYE with his parents and their friends, I was dreading it but at least it was an easy way to spend the Holiday.

New Year's Eve 2007 included two events- the first part of the day was spent traveling from Seattle to Mount Snoqualmie to have a picnic in the Sarah Anna and to celebrate the Russian New Year. It was a fun experience of driving to Sarah Anna with a large dog in the trunk, arriving and standing and shivering in the cold while the men and women drank tea and vodka and counted down the year in Russia finishing it by popping champagne. I spent my time talking to the kids and ignoring the adults, wandering around in the Sarah Anna Anna and letting the conversations flow around me-I don't speak Russian so speaking wasn't required of me. Going into 2008 was spent attending a Russian party near Seattle, we drove to the event by ourselves electing to meet his parents there. Once we arrived and entered the party I had my first experience of a culture shock, we were in the United States, we were in the Seattle area, but this was a piece of Russia mixed with Ukraine, the party was filled with people sitting at assigned tables, the tables were lined with bottles of champagne and vodka with a few bottles of water placed throughout. We found our table and sat next to his parents, I was a little over 12 weeks pregnant and barely showing, people began drinking almost immediately and I got water in my glass as soon as I could only to be told constantly that it was not proper to do toasts with water. Luckily people drinking fast lose interest in those who aren't drinking and focus on themselves so I kept drinking my water and watching the people around me. We arrived at the party at 9 pm and for 3 hours people ate, drank, drank more, ate more food, talked louder and louder shouting over one another and shortly before midnight began dancing. As midnight hit people truly got crazy in their dancing and drinking falling over one another, shouting, but they were happy in their drunkenness, I, on the other hand, was counting down until I could beg to leave. I was the designated driver and I had never felt so desperate to leave a place in my life, my Igor was drunk, and I was tired.

New Year's day dawned bright and early and thankfully we had arrived at home, the Igor stumbled inside the house and passed out quickly without too much throwing up or acting out like a drunkard typically does. The Igor woke up with a hangover and not happy to have to face the sun and his hangover, I, on the other hand, was planning to go to my parents to eat black-eyed peas and cheese cake-a tradition we have developed for many years that supposedly would mean good luck in the new year. I don't know if it does, but I was happy to escape way from the Igor and spent my day with my family.

Married woman takes on 2008

As January continued on in the new year I was counting down the days until I would be able to go into my new obstetrician's office for an ultrasound, I was focusing on the pregnancy. The Igor has stopped coming with me to appointments, he was tired of feigning interest, he expressed doubts about the baby is his, and we started having daily arguments. He spent his evenings drinking and getting high with his friends, smoking cigarette after cigarette and I spent my days with my mom, visiting my dad at his office when he was working locally, and spending time with my brother and my niece. I developed a routine of waiting till the Igor left for the day, calling my parents seeing who wanted to hang out and going and spending the day and early evening with them coming home in time to cook dinner that was never appreciated and often criticized.

February passed by with no big issues, Valentine was a lackluster holiday but the Igor made an effort with a homemade card which was sweet except for the painful smile on his face that ruined the gesture. March was coming and with it, I could finally find out if I was having a boy or girl, I was going to be having a birthday, and my ex had convinced the Igor to move into our spare bedroom. I was dreading sharing the house with a messy ex-bf, but I was trying to stay positive. Halfway through March, I learned that I was having a boy, I was happy, the baby was healthy and big and developing well. The ex-boyfriend moved into our house and brought with him his mess though he limited it to his bedroom. And my birthday was coming fast, my Igor decided that he was going to throw my ex a party since his birthday was a few days after mine and so party preparations began. It was going to be a big Russian birthday party filled with music, vodka, strobe lights, and a fog machine.

March 26 was the date of the party, the house was cleaned, furniture arranged, my laptop was set up and ready to be used, the alcohol was bought, and snacks were ready to be served. I was 6 months pregnant and my belly was a perfect pregnant woman's belly. I was apprehensive about the party since I would be the only sober person amongst a group of drunk or drinking people, but I steeled my resolve to survive the party. The party began and people began drinking, Russian guy after a guy showed upbringing with them friends, the music was turned loud, and my Igor went out to warn and invite the neighbors to our party so that they wouldn't call the cops on us. The party grew louder and people drank more and more, I had lost track of where my Igor was, I was tired of people drinking and knocking drinks and food on the floor, I was talking with some girls in the kitchen when I heard a noise and went out to realize my Igor's friend had dropped my laptop and was laughing about it. He told me it was shit anyway and to get over it. I was so upset, people were drinking and dropping garbage everywhere, girls were dancing and guys were drooling over them, I couldn't breathe I was so hurt and angry, and lonely. And then to top off the evening of misery I finally saw my Igor among the people, he was sitting on our couch with his arm around a woman, they were laughing and smiling and whispering to each other. I was so angry and hurt, it was my shared birthday party and this is what he was doing, he was drunk and flirting with another woman. I marched over to him and pulled her up, I shoved her away from him, found the guys she had came with and told them to get her out of my house, I had caused a scene and some women rushed to my side, telling me to calm down but I couldn't. I hit my Igor in his face and went to my room, I packed a bag and called my parents who were sleeping. I told them I would be coming home, I couldn't stay at my house and I left. This is what my life had become, misery, anger, hurt, I had ruined my life, I had quit my job, I was going to be a mom and I hated my life.

In April I was scheduled to have a baby shower- a day to celebrate becoming a mom, to have people over, to acknowledge the fact we were having a son due in June. I was dreading it, I had come back home but life was awkward, it was forced and I didn't see how it was going to improve. I knew I had made a mistake at getting married, but I didn't have an escape and I had chosen this so I had to stick with it. The baby shower was being jointly hosted by my mom and his mom which meant his parents would be having alcohol for the guest, and my parents would choose the cake and games, I was just happy my mom and dad were going to becoming. The baby shower day arrived and it was a fun experience, my parents were there, my dad as always providing humor when he could see I wasn't happy, my niece there crying non stop as she didn't like strangers and was not the happiest babies, and my Igor and his parents were there opening bottles of alcohol and drinking as they did it seemed on every occasion and party.

After the baby shower, I began counting down the days until I could have the baby-it seemed so distant yet so close, 6 weeks until my due date but I knew I couldn't wait that long. I spent each evening alone in the house while my Igor went out drinking with his friends, getting high, and I would google how to get ready for childbirth. I was cleaning, preparing items, and putting together baby items in preparation. I had prepared my hospital bag, and with enough distraction, an additional 3 weeks passed in a blur. By mid-May, I was walking nonstop, and eventually, June came along, June 10 happened like any other day. I woke up, ate, walked, talked with my parents, the Igor went to work, came home, went to his friends to party assuring me he would be home sometime later. I was having stomach pains so I took a bath, I knew what it was but I was alone, so I just sat in the bathtub for hours, running the bath each time it got the cold feeling the contractions coming closer together. I called my parents but they were sleeping, it was after midnight and the Igor wasn't home, he wasn't answering his phone. I was scared, but I kept waiting, he eventually came home after 1 is, I was having contractions 4 minutes apart and the doctor was notified I would be coming into the hospital. He drove me to the hospital, drunk, high, fast, and in a manner of minutes we arrived, I was rushed to Labor and Delivery where they asked me what my birth plan was, asked if I wanted pain medicine, and who I would want in the room with me. Eventually, my family showed up, and I was given an epidural, as soon as the epidural was administered the rate of the baby's heart plummeted. His life was in danger, terms were thrown at me, and in the end, I was rushed in to get an emergency C-section. Getting rushed into the operation room I was terrified, the bright lights, having my hands strapped down to a cold metal table, a barrier was put up so that I couldn't see my stomach, them injecting me with a spinal block so that I couldn't feel the bottom half of my body followed by them informing me I would feel pressure. What does that even mean? Pressure. Turns out pressure means it feels like someone is jumping on top of you and you can't breathe, then you hearing cutting sounds, and finally the sound of a baby crying, at some point I passed out, I was eventually sewn back up, and sent back to a room where I came awake after some time and the world was this magical happy place, and I even had a baby. I was high, the spinal block was morphine, the epidural was a concoction of pain meds, I could barely feel my fingers, and when they handed over my son, I didn't have the strength to hold him but I was supposed to so I tried.

The first time I held my son was this oddly magical moment, I was high, I couldn't feel my legs, and I was a mom, they were entrusting me to watch over this tiny life when I couldn't even feel my legs. They started instructing me to feed him with my breasts, to hold him against my skin, but they didn't seem to understand the fact that I was on a different level. I could feel nothing, I couldn't get my son to eat because I couldn't use my arms. My son who we had decided to name Danny didn't eat for the first day, by the second day they were pushing me to use formula, but I refused, I had come down off of the clouds and I was aware, awake, and I refused to give him a bottle. Their next suggestion was to have me pump my breasts to get the milk supply going, so feeling like a cow that's what I attempted to do, I have no idea who was with me during the first few days other than my mom being a steady support for me, the Igor left for work, my mom was worried about the baby not eating and gradually got pushier. But I persisted and eventually, he latched onto my breast and drank milk. That night the nurse informed me I would have to start walking-I hadn't walked since the C-section and judging by the limited movement in the bed it was going to be a painful experience. The baby went to the nursery and I was helped out of bed and told that I needed to use the washroom and then walk for 10 minutes. Moving from the bed to the washroom felt like I was being punched in the abdomen, it was excruciating and using the washroom was even worse than the walking. For the first time in my life I cried while walking, I cried while using the washroom, the stitches caused pain, the staples in my stomach ached and felt foreign, and I couldn't use the washroom. After 10 minutes I was exhausted and fell asleep in the bed, I was woken up a few hours later to feed the baby then once again fell asleep until my mom arrived in the morning. I stayed in the hospital for 3 days, for 3 days I was told to use the washroom, to walk, to move, and throughout those days the pain was part of my world, they began giving me pain pills to help, all they did was cause me to fall asleep. On the third day, they removed the staples, they watching me in the washroom and nodded their approval that my bladder and organs were functioning, and I was sent home with my son who was safely secured in his car seat. My Igor came to pick me up complaining to the nurses about me having to be in a wheelchair, but eventually, he acquiesced and I was allowed to leave with our son. We drove to our house- we had a week previously moved to a new place, but it was a move in the process still happening, luckily we had the basics set up. My mom met us there to help me while the Igor returned to work- my mom and I had never been closer, she supported me as I adapted to being a mom, cared for the baby as I slept off the pain pills. The wound was healing but it would take time, the baby weight hadn't magically fallen off while in the hospital so I was exhausted, depressed, and dealing with pain. Postpartum depression was very real for me, but it was unacceptable, I had to suck it up. My mom had an idea for her, my dad, the baby, and I to travel 3 hours away to the ocean to celebrate the baby's first birthday. I jumped at it. The only help I was receiving at home was from my parents so I looked forward to taking a trip with them.

Life as a new mom

The trip to Oregon and the beach was a fun experience, it felt so good to get away from the Igor and to just focus on being a new mom, and have help nonstop. My parents were jewels, my dad had taken an instant love to Danny and would spend hours holding him, soothing him, spoiling him rotten, my dad was an amazing grandpa and loved having the weekend with his newest grandson. We went to the beach, went to dinners where on a dare my dad suggested I order razor clams- that was an awful experience, I love seafood but that was a whole new seafood experience, and I learned about a clam that I didn't like, but it provided humor and I laughed like I hadn't laughed in months. The weekend passed by quickly and soon we were on our way back to our homes. I returned home to our house much as we left it, and to Igor who spent his free time drinking, smoking, using weed, numbing out and hanging out with his friends, and I returned to doing things by myself.

One day when Danny was about 1.5 months old I guess the Igor was filled with remorse, guilt, or pity he decided to start hosting his parties in our garage so that he could at least feign being there for me, so his friends and he would come to our home at 7 in the evening, smoke, drink, play cards while sitting in the garage. They were loud, annoying, and by midnight right when the baby awoke for his feeding they would start asking for me to cook for them-or worse they would ravage the kitchen making a mess everywhere that I would have to clean up in the morning. In July 2008 my Igor's parents decided to host a friend's daughter at their house for the Summer as well as my Igor's grandmother. The in-laws invited my Igor and me over to their house for dinner and to meet them. We arrived with Danny and introductions were made, his grandma was a nice elderly lady who spoke no English and the girl, Katya, was a skinny 18-year-old girl who spoke limited English and enjoyed smiling at my Igor. I hated her immediately, but I was polite, smiled, and tried to engage her in conversation. His grandma started asking questions about how I breastfed my son, and at one point pulled down my shirt to look at my breasts-I vowed to lock myself in the bathroom rather than risk a second experience such as that. Summer was in full motion, the parties at our house had increased to all 7 days a week versus only being 5 days a week, especially as we had a commodity of having to invite the Russian girl to our house to hang out with us. I am not sure how it happened but we had gained the responsibility of entertaining her, in exchange Igor's parents asked to watch Danny on Saturday nights, so with reluctance, I introduced him to the bottle and would pump milk for him to drink. My Igor was happy he was trying to hook his friends up with Katya, and I would hear about their planning and games and resolve myself to watching. I grew sick of it, I had just had a baby, I was being ignored, everyone's focus was on this girl, I didn't get help with the baby, and I was expected to be okay with a girl constantly hanging out with my Igor at our house. I lost my patience one Saturday night when I was shunned to the kitchen to cook for everyone, I said fuck it, I vowed to stop breastfeeding and I opened up a bottle of beer and drank for the first time in over a year, it tasted amazing so I drank a second beer. I got angry, I was frustrated, lonely, and sad, I was sick of being disrespected and so when Igor came inside from the garage to check on dinner, and to see how I was doing, I informed him that Katya was not staying the night as he had previously asked, he argued with me and in the end told me she was, so I waited until he was about to pass out, I took her purse and threw it outside, I kicked his friends out, and I locked her outside. She wanted to flirt with all of them then surely she could figure out where she was going to sleep, we had a barn with a mattress so worst case she could rest there. I went to bed and woke up with a hangover, the two beers had made my headache.

When I woke up, the first thing I remembered was locking out Katya from the house, the second thing was that my head was hurting, and thirdly I was so upset with my Igor for putting me in such a position. How could someone do this to someone they lived with, had taken vows with, how could they treat someone this way. I realized that it was my fault, I had forced him into marriage, I had trapped him, and he was just taking his revenge on me, it was to be expected so I vowed to never feel this way again. I devised a plan, anytime on the weekends his friends came over I would invite their girlfriends-we weren't close but hey women appreciate being included in things, I bought beer and the next weekend I got drunk with the women and hose as I commonly referred to Katya kept her distance from the guys. The summer continued, we had parties at our place Friday and Saturday nights, and I adopted a new friend, she and I were both moms and we both hated Katya for taking the attention of our partners away from us. We formed a friendship of sorts where we would drink, get wasted, flirt with each other, neither of us was gay or lesbian but we enjoyed talking, laughing, and causing our partners to stare at us, we reached a mutual agreement of drinking till we could bear to kiss each other and at that point our guys would remember us and pay us attention.

We were young, stupid, cruel, instead of blaming our guys for being assholes, we blamed a young foreign girl, we dumped beer on her head, at one point my friend smacked the girl in her face, it got more dramatic until the day we reached a breaking point and locked everyone outside on a Saturday night and her and I got wasted and watched movies laughing at all of them.

A somber winter

A few weeks later Katya went back to Russia along with Igor's grandma, things went back to normal- I started hanging out with my brother on the weekends while my parent's or Igor's watched Danny, and Igor spent the weekends hanging out with his friends, sometimes we would hang out together but usually it was solo adventures. My brother and I would get high and drink, I would drink primarily and he would focus on weed and booze equally. At some point, I would sober up enough to drive the 10 minutes to my house to pass out and wake up on a Saturday or Sunday morning to make breakfast and hang out for a few hours during the day with the Igor.

Halloween was approaching and soon after would be the Igor's birthday, his friends and he were planning to throw parties for both occasions, I was excited but also dreading these events.

The parties would be held in the friend's house of his basement where they had a party room, billiards room, and relatively soundproof walls. I steeled myself up to the occasion of the first party, I was going to dress as a witch whereas the Igor was dressing up by shaving his head and acting as racist as possible. We went to a Halloween party at a friend's place, the Igor adopted his usual attitude when he was around his friends which basically meant he ignored me, acted dismissive of me, acted like men were everything and women were little more than sexual objects to speak rudely too. I was upset but trying not to show it, our son was off with his grandparents as usual, and I was drinking shot after shot of vodka and trying to maintain my composure. At one point I had reached the threshold of being drunk, the guy's girlfriend and I were lonely, the party was mainly guys who it felt like went to smoke cigarettes every 5 minutes so we decided to take matters into our own hands and   ourselves by kissing and making out-it had worked once so surely it would work again, sure enough it did, we weren't into it but at least we got the attention of the partiers. The party at that point passed in a blur of drunken kisses and stupid words falling from our lips, and at the end of the party, we promised to never do it again.

The next party was 2 weeks away, the guy's birthdays were one day apart and they were excited to throw another party, I was even more apprehensive than I was before, I was tired of parties, of being ignored, of being told what to do. The night of the party I decided to pregame in preparation of it, by the time I finished getting dressed I was drunk, once we arrived at the party I was pissed off, drunk, and not in the mood to be there, so I drank more, I blacked out, and the next day I woke up. My Igor was furious with me, I had started a fight with him, I threw a drink at him, and yelled at him-I was an embarrassment and I was no longer allowed to drink around him. So last night's fight continued into the next day only now I was sober, hungover, and miserable and afraid to tell him what a lousy person he was so I just listened with resignation as his words tumbled out at me. It became a trend for a while, we would go to one of his friend's parties, I would drink, I would get drunk and say anything I was feeling, often about how miserable I was, and he would get upset at me the next day. Liquid courage gave me the freedom , to be honest with what was going on, but it made me depressed and unable to function in the day to day things. Thanksgiving was approaching and I was excited it was going to be my first year as a mom and I volunteered our house to host a gigantic Thomas/Howard family reunion feast. I became obsessed with it, what we were going to cook, who was invited, what would be the activities, to relax the night before Thanksgiving my Igor and I went with my cousins to hang out at my brother Chris' house where we were planning to drink, relax, and chill out. It started out as a good time, as usual, Chris drank fast and a lot, but he had a match between my cousins and I who could all drink a lot, then add in Igor, and we got wasted fast, Chris and the Igor smoked weed to add in the relaxing effect, and soon they all went out to smoke cigarettes, while I stayed inside with Chris' wife. Eventually they came back inside drunk, smelling of cigarettes, and weed, laughing, loud and full of jubilance that only drunk people get right before they reach their edge-sure enough 10 minutes later I was ready to go home, Igor said something that offended Chris, and the cousins were starving so we made our goodbyes and started out the door, by this time I was drunk, Igor went to start the car, he was going to drive us all; I forgot something inside Chris's house so I went back to get it only to have him yell at me, pushing me, and slam the door in my face causing me to fall down and Igor who was walking up to see where I was at saw my brother shoving me and slamming his door shut got furious, rammed the door open and punched my brother in his face. I was shocked and upset- Thanksgiving was tomorrow and we had to get along. I am not sure what would have happened if I hadn't thought to cry at that point, but luckily I started crying distracting the men and I was escorted home where we all went to bed.

Thanksgiving morning started with the doorbell ringing at 7 am, my parents arriving to start cooking turkeys, bringing with them pounds of potatoes, carrots, sausages, and many pies, it was going to be an all-day cooking event and it was starting now- hangover or not. So leaving Igor sleeping, I began the prep work of preparing the 4 turkeys with my dad, preparing the stuffing, peeling potatoes, carrots, chopping celery, and generally figuring out how much we needed of each thing. Eventually my brother Chris arrived wearing his broken glasses and carrying with him a crap attitude which my mom set out to warn him sternly to knock it off- he could be angry after Thanksgiving but we have family comings, aunts, uncles, cousins from both sides of the family and today was not the day to act like an asshole. He swallowed his anger and cooking continued, at one point all the kids and grandkids were taken outside to take photos on the trampoline, it was not what I would call a fun experience but we survived it. Our house was jam-packed with 30 people all who loved to eat, add in the kids and we were pushing 50 people total. Finally the turkeys were finished and within 2 minutes the family had picked every scrap of meat off the bone, cleaned out the potatoes, dressing, green beans so that by the time my parents and I were finished cooking, we had only a minimal amount of food to choose from but it was worth it, having this large Thanksgiving that brought everyone together and it turns out it was the last largest Thanksgiving my grandmother, my dad's mom would experience in her lifetime.

After Thanksgiving came Christmas and with Christmas came the usual maniacal behavior of shopping, decorations, festivities, Danny was older so I got to show him Christmas lights, let him visit Santa, and overall Christmas became enjoyable, though he was still too young to open presents and was more fascinated by boxes than anything else, it was fun spending the day with my parents. My dad especially made Christmas come to life he was the glue for our family and so it was a treat to spend it with him. On New Year's Eve, was spent in the Sarah Anna Anna just like the year before and afterward we dropped Danny off with the grandparents and went to Igor's friends party where they were cooking kebabs and other traditional Russian dishes, I had agreed to not drink more than a glass of champagne at midnight, so I counted down all night enduring all of the lame music, and drunk guys falling down- once midnight hit Igor passed out and I celebrated with a glass of champagne followed by a few beers that his friends pushed on me, then I too stumbled to bed and slept nicely until the morning. New Year's day was spent relaxing, Igor had a hangover so it was a quiet morning and the afternoon was spent with his parents celebrating the holiday. The next few years followed the same pattern, Russian girl coming to visit, Igor's mom flying off to Russia, Igor ignoring me, I got used to it, and the drinking numbed the feelings on the weekends.

3 Years later

Christmas is approaching and 2011 is coming to an end, Igor and I have reached a point in our marriage where we're both clearly unhappy-he's filled with resentments and angry at being married, I've started drinking more to cope with him, he's either embarrassed by me, or he can't get enough of me, I've lost all the weight from having Danny courtesy of a stringent diet of throwing up a minimum of 5 times a day and only drinking light beer with a few shots of vodka thrown in. My emotions were starting to get worse, I was closer than ever before with my dad- he spent hours confiding in me in regards to what was going on with mom, her gambling, her writing fraudulent checks, her sinking them further into debt causing him to have to work 60-80 hours a week, his exhaustion at having to travel to the Philippines, Korea, Thailand all the time, his wanting to just buy a Harley motorcycle and settle down, but she just constantly needs more money and he is tired. He's hiding his friends from her, his smoking weed and coming to my house to hang out and share a 6 pack-if you asked me, I would happily then and now tell you my dad was my best friend. He listened to me as I confided in him about my regret of marriage, my fears, my sadness at my life, he stressed he was worried about the pattern of my drinking, worrying I was starting to drink too much. But he knew and I knew I wasn't going to stop drinking, I was stressed, I was miserable and it was my only outlet and he could understand that that's why he smoked weed, that's why we shared a 6 pack.

A few days after Christmas my mom and dad flew down to San Diego, he was working on a Navy boat project and they needed him there for the next few months, he couldn't leave mom behind cause she might gamble, and she was finally in a better place, she had attended a Gamblers anonymous meetings and he was hopeful. In Washington we got hit with a major Sarah

Anna Annastorm; I couldn't go to their house to check on the dog though they had generously let me use their car-my car had broken down years ago and Igor wasn't ready to fix it or buy me a new one. The storm got worse, it was Sarah Anna Annaing so heavily, it was freezing nightly before it got too terrible I took a chance and stocked the house with groceries, and wood and two nights later the storm got so bad that Igor was forced to stay home from work. The roads couldn't be driven on, during the day it would Sarah Anna Anna and at night it would freeze turning everything to ice. We lost power and had to rely on our fireplace for heat and to keep us warm, around the time we lost power we lost cell phone service and internet. My parents had no way to contact me and they were worried sick so worried that they took the initiative to contact the local sheriff's department and ask them to send out a sheriff for a wellness check, my dad who had spoken to me only a day or two before knew I was having a rough week with Igor, and he had told me to breathe, that I should divorce Igor and come home and live with my parents-it may be rough at first but I was young-there was still time for me, I could go back to school and they would help me-I just had to slow down my drinking, then I could be a great mom, have a career, and be happy again. I didn't know what to tell him-I just told him I would think on it, I'm just so scared. Then we hung up and he didn't hear from me, the sheriff checked on us and then let my parents know I was okay, that was January 19, 2012. January 20, 2012, dawned with no power, no cell phone, no connection, by mid-morning had gotten power back on thankfully- I could charge my laptop and it seemed we had internet so I could post on facebook that we were safe, warm, and okay, I was scrolling through Facebook when I noticed my cousin had posted something about a favorite uncle dying unexpectedly. We only have two uncles so I selfishly hoped she was talking about our Uncle John, but I had this sinking sensation, I saw our neighbor outside and asked him if I could borrow his phone to call my mom. My hands were shaking, my breathing was fast, but I got through to her, she was crying hysterically and for the first and only time in my life did my knees go weak and I lose the ability to stand, I didn't faint I just lost all ability in that moment, my dad had had a heart attack, he was working on a ship in San Diego and was talking to a crew member about a problem with the radar and the next moment they told me he was clutching his chest. He fell down, just like I did, they tried to restart his heart on the way to the hospital, but they couldn't. My daddy died on January 20, 2012, my heart broke for the first time in my life on January 20, 2012, what was this world without my dad. My best friend. My confidant, the man who showed me how to change tires, change the oil on a car, the man who listened and told me the straight answer though I never wanted to hear it, and didn't always follow it, the man who was the peacemaker in our family. My dad was gone and eventually, I started breathing again. Danny was scared, Igor came to know what happened and for the first time in what felt like forever, he was kind to me.

Part 2

One day I got sick and tired of being sick and tired, I fought my way out of misery so deep that life seemed impossible to live, from being institutionalized, emotionally bankrupt, and hated by what felt everyone, I began to climb my way out of the pits of addiction. Over 3 years ago I went from being a drunk, not present woman, angry, depressed, anxious, a shell of a person to an outgoing, recovering out loud woman who hosts recovery groups, coaches those seeking a substance-free life, hosting a podcast, and a woman helping to show others how to live in the light. - Jouikov, CPC, CPRC, SRDC

Dead Father, Life Over

The next few days passed in a blur, I arranged for my mom to fly home immediately, I drove to the airport to pick her up, I didn't drink because I knew once I started I wouldn't stop. My dad was 51 how could he be dead! I got my mom, got the dog and brought them both to my house, my mom popped some sleeping pills and slept as best as she could. The next day she drove herself home and grieved, I called various funeral homes in San Diego and found one, we had to have my dad packaged properly to be flown home to Washington, I found a funeral home in Washington to receive his body and that would help us to arrange his funeral. I drove my mom to the funeral home, we went over funeral packages, these vultures asking for thousands of dollars from a new widow who had not planned a death, let alone had that much money laying around. Eventually, we worked it out, I arranged through my Igor to give her the money to pay for the funeral until the life insurance money came in, we set a date for the funeral, we submitted the obituary, and we invited people to come. As per a traditional southern funeral, we would have a wake with hours for the family the day before the actual funeral- I was to give the eulogy.

By the time Friday rolled around the family had arrived in droves, cousins, aunts, uncles, my grandmother, all of my brothers, and they all expected to meet up and hang out with me, with my other brother Chris. I was exhausted and hanging on by a thread- a thread of drinking just enough beer to numb, but not too much where I fall drunk. I was exhausted, I was numb, I wanted it over with. Igor drove him and me to the funeral home to view my dad, walking up to my dad's casket and looking inside was a life-changing moment. Here was the man who had let me sleep on his chest when I was a little girl, here was the man who taught me to drive, to change tires, oil, who taught me to have more self respect, here was the guy whose last words were to get divorced, be happy, and here he was dead, he had suffered so much, he had been so unhappy, and look where it had landed him. His body was stiff, he was bloated, he was pale, he was wearing his favorite shirt, his face looked different, he looked so alone, and just like that the numbness facade started to crack, I started crying that day-but I wasn't ready, I needed to get through the funeral before I could feel. I drank more beer, and I smoked weed, I relaxed and finished out the wake, cousins, brothers, and I all went back to Chris's house to drink and hang out, to numb out.

Saturday rolled around, January 27 exactly 1 week since my dad had died and we were going to put him in the ground, he was ex-military so the Navy would be playing the trumpet in honor of him. We arrived at the funeral home, sober, sad, and mentally as prepared as one could be in this situation. I had my black suit on, I had declined makeup, I had drunk a beer, used mouth freshener, and I knew what I was going to say. 11 am came and in walked person after person, walking to the front to shake my mom's hand, or hug her, and me, and the family, uncles, aunts, cousins, co-workers, managers, friends, person after person, there had to be at least 100 people or more there, people who my dad had spoken to, be friends with, an uncle to. At 1130 it was my turn to go to the front, it was time for my speech, I walked up to the podium, I looked out in front of me making eye contact with each person who had come.

"Thank you all for coming out to honor Colin Marion Thomas, he was a good man, a good dad, as you all have noticed he impacted many lives in a variety of ways, Colin was born on June 28, 1959 he was the youngest son of Anna and Virgil Thomas, the brother to 2 older sisters, and an older brother, he is the youngest and the first to leave this world. He was loved by all. He was the father to Benjamin, Oliver, Christopher, and Britney, the grandfather of 10 grandkids, he loved spending time watching football, hanging out with his friends, and cracking open a cold beer. He was an amazing father and my best friend, he was the one who was always there to listen no matter what.....” I broke up at that point, I couldn't remember what I was going to say, I started crying and I couldn't go on, my Uncle took over, he and my dad had never had a great relationship but he stepped up and helped out. After the eulogies we prepared to carry my dad out, my mom had changed her mind-she didn't want me to carry my dad instead she decided that it should be all men who carried him, but I reminded her that Igor and dad didn't get along and it should be his daughter who he taught to be strong to help carry him to the Hearst; she relented and away we carried him, he was put inside the Hearst and driven to his final resting ground.

I chose to walk to his resting place, it was a short walk up the hill, it also gave me the opportunity to share a beer with my brothers and one of my uncles, it was much needed for what was about to happen. I got an opportunity to speak to my dad's best friends, 2 women he had spent hours with when he was in town, and it was one of the best moments of the entire sad day. Once we walked to the gravesite, my dad was situated above the hole in the ground; the trumpeters played the tune, a final prayer was said, and my dad was lowered into the ground. My mom was taken back down the hill for the traditional mourning feast, and my brothers and I eventually followed. People sat around at tables and ate food, I had brought ribs I had made and pulled pork, people laughed and talked, they ate and ate, and didn't they realize my dad was dead, I was so upset but I had to put on a smile and pretend everything was fine. It was miserable, it was so hard, talking to my dad's coworkers, my dad's old manager who said they were going to name a training center after my dad in the next few months and to reach out if we needed anything, all I needed was my dad back but that was impossible so I nodded and thanked him. Eventually, people finished eating and by mutual consent my uncles, cousins, brothers, and I went to my mom's house to drink and spend a few more hours together. Once there we popped the bottles of beer open, mixing beer with whiskey, whiskey with vodka, vodka with wine, and wine with beer, it was a deadly combination, my duty was done, the numbing wasn't working anymore and I needed oblivion, I drank shot after shot, beer after beer, wine glass after wine glass, my son was with Igor's parents and he went briefly to check on them, he knew I wasn't going to stop drinking that night no matter what so he didn't even ask me to. I stopped counting how much I drank after I drank the 12th beer and the 10th shot of alcohol, I don't remember how much wine I drank. At some point I blacked out, I was cracking jokes with my uncle and aunt who knew what I was doing, their son had died many years earlier and they used alcohol to numb themselves, so they matched me drink for drink and let me talk crap and act a fool, they kept expecting me to throw up, but I couldn't, I just kept drinking until eventually I passed out on the floor, Igor picked me threw me in his car and took me home. I slept on the couch that night and woke up the next day dehydrated but shockingly alive despite the amount of alcohol I drank.

The day after the funeral I met up with my family for lunch, I was hungover and drinking hair of the dog to combat the hangover feeling, I was taking it slow too fast would mean throwing up, so I took my time drinking my first two beers, and eventually the shakes went away and I was sober enough to drive to my family. We hung out, they talked to me about the things I had said when I was drunk and I kindly reminded them that I wouldn't be reflecting on anything I said the night before. I ate lunch, and eventually, Igor and I went to his parent's house to pick up Danny, they told me how sorry they were for my loss, his mom's mom had died a year before so she could understand, I thanked them, and we ate dinner together. I asked them to watch Danny another night, I was hungover, and I wasn't done drinking, I wasn't ready to feel anything, I wasn't ready to mourn or be in grief. They agreed and I went to my brothers where we decided we would drive to my dad's gravesite to drink beer and smoke weed. I hated smoking weed, it made me paranoid and tired but I agreed. We drank beer, sat and talked and eventually we went back home, I went back to my house after dropping him home, I drank once home until I passed out. The next day I got sober enough to function, but I hated feeling, I hated crying, feeling sad, facing the truth that my dad was dead. My mom was barely functioning but I couldn't bear to call her. I couldn't bear to face her, she needed someone but I was angry at her and couldn't bear to hear her voice.

Beer became my crutch, it became my coping mechanism, it was the solution to all of the world's problems I had been struggling to deal with, struggling to accept, struggling with in every way, I had fallen in love with a new thing, the feeling of being truly numb-something I had experienced throughout my dad's funeral was now an option for day to day life. The moment I started numbing instead of grieving I had made a decision to stop growing as a person. I had made the decision to stop fully experiencing life, I was tired of it, tired of the pain, I hated my mom, I hated my family, my friend was dead, and while I loved being a mother I was so tired, I was tired of the mental head games of a hateful marriage, I was tired of feeling. I was depressed, and drinking helped me to numb out, to take a break from the world. I would love to say my life didn't go bad, that the blissful numbing out solved all my problems-but if that were true, what would be the point of this story. I was 23 years old, almost 24, I had been married for almost 4 years, I had a son who was 4 who had also lost the man he was closest to, his grandpa, and I was miserable. I was lost, confused, and uncertain how to continue, so logically I began drinking more and more.

On February 20 it was officially one month since my dad died, I arranged with my brother to meet up at my dad's graveside to share a beer (or 5) and then go hang out at his house, the kids would hang out together, and we could kick it. It was the start of what would become a pattern, drive to my brother's house, buy beer, let Danny and his cousin play together, drink beer, my brother would smoke weed, watch movies, make food, sober up, and drive back home. It was our thrice-weekly thing to do, sometimes it was during the day, other times I would ride with Igor as he went to hang out with his click of friends. It continued in the same pattern, day after day, wake up drink a beer, make food, hang out with my brother, sometimes call my mom, and other times just stay at home, color with Danny, mow the grass, lay on the couch, but the constant was I never could run out of beer.

March came and it was my birthday, I was turning 24 years old, my Igor was going to hang out with his friends-to him it was just another day, I asked my mom to watch Danny, and I went to my brother's house and got drunk-not so drunk where I had no memory, just drunk enough to feel nothing. I was supposed to be the designated driver- which is funny since it was my birthday but I was just happy to be out, so when the Igor called, I drank some water, opened my eyes wide, and drove to get him, I was somewhat sober, I knew how to drive after a few drinks, pay attention to the lane, pay attention to the surroundings, don't look at the phone-oops I looked at the phone, and sure enough I bumped a car beside me, I was terrified, what a way to ensure you're sober, I had knocked his side mirror off of his Lexus, he was going to be so angry, but I just drove and picked him up. He had been drinking and smoking weed so he didn't notice at first, we started driving and I started feeling sleepy, he asked me to pull over and started screaming at me, I mutely let him finish driving us home. I was ashamed, he was upset, it was not the best birthday I'd ever had.

Drinking became my priority, it was the thing I lived for, I would mother to the best of my intoxicated ability throughout the day, I would make some form of food, and I would attempt to at least pretend to clean something, do some type of laundry, then I would lay on the couch lost in a drunken stupor. I stopped talking to people, my head was the only safe place to be, a place where there were no judgments, a place where I could feel nothing. I stopped sleeping at night unless I was drunk, I would pass out next to Danny on his bed, I would wake in the morning to an angry Igor who would speed off to work. The Igor began a new strategy of threats, threatening to take away money, take away the phone, the internet, he couldn't take the car because the car was my mom's car she had given to me to use, but everything else he could take he took. I tried to pull myself out of my depression but I just felt so hopeless, I was sad, lonely, drinking helped but then it stopped helping. By Summer life was a miserable pit- the only uplifting moment was organizing Danny's 4th birthday party at an inflatable bounce house, it got me energized and excited for the first time in months, but it passed by as quickly as it had come.

Suicidal Thinking

Igor's little patience was fast fading, the taking away of items wasn't working and by the end of July, he began threatening me of cheating on me if I didn't stop drinking. I couldn't stop drinking it was the only way to survive life, I needed the beer, I needed the numbness, I had started drinking in the mornings, in the afternoons, in the evenings at night once the Igor was home and locked in his computer room. He rarely spoke to me, he never offered to help me, his help was through threats, he didn't understand how I could be so impacted by the loss of my dad, why couldn't I get over it. He didn't get it, he didn't get me, so I just drank more, there was a point in the world but I couldn't remember it. I couldn't remember that I was a mom, that it wasn't only about me, that I loved someone else. I could remember sometimes, but it was a floating thought that would drift to the surface only occasionally-enough where I was able to function, but dim enough where I could focus solely on drinking. August came and with it a large argument with Igor, he was sick of me being depressed, sick of my drinking, he threatened again to cheat, he was angry, domineering, scary, I was tired of it all so I drank more than I ever had before, it made what I drank the night of my dad's funeral look tame, I mixed vodka, whiskey, wine, beer, sake, and I drank, I added in some sleeping pills, Tylenol, and anti-nausea pills because I was so tired, I couldn't sleep, my head hurt, and I was so tired, I was trying to kill myself. I got scared and called my mom, I told her what I had done, she called Igor, and he called the paramedics. I was rushed to the hospital in front of Danny who thankfully only saw the firetruck and got excited, once at the hospital my mom came and got Danny-she would bring him to my in-laws the next day to go to the beach with them. I was admitted overnight in the hospital they didn't have to pump my stomach, but they did give me multiple shots into the belly button, and I had to drink charcoal. I was asked what happened, was I trying to die. I assured every nurse, every doctor, that I didn't want to die I just didn't realize the number of pills cause I had drunk, it was a simple silly mistake-somehow they believed me. The next day another nurse came and spoke to me, she explained how she had been in an abusive relationship for years- she drank to numb herself, she thought she wasn't worth anything, she almost lost everything but no man is worth drinking ourselves to death over. She gave me a therapist's phone number and finally agreed to release me to go home, I was free at last and I could not wait to get out of there. Igor was coming to pick me up and we were going to drive down to Ocean Beach in Oregon to celebrate his mom's birthday.

Once we got to Oregon we reached the agreement to never speak about what I did-no mention of suicide it was her birthday and we weren't going to ruin it by mentioning my insanity. I agreed we were going to begin the act of pretending nothing happened; this was going to be the trend for the upcoming months. Once we returned from the beach Igor and I got into a habit-don't talk about the suicide attempt, allow Britney to go to therapy, and send our son off to the grandparents on the weekends. On the weekends I would see how much beer I could drink in the span of 2 days, and on Sundays, we would go for dinner at Igor's parents' house and pretend everything was fine. My drinking was growing, it was beginning to get out of control, my brother too was spiraling out of control, he had added in weekend shoplifting binges, he would run across the street steal cases of beer, then spend the weekend drinking them-I never asked at the time how he came by the beer-I didn't want to know, but deep down I suspected because he wouldn't go into the store across the street; whatever he was doing I was happy to not have to financially back his drinking and happy to have a scapegoat such as him to compare my own drinking too. As long as he drank and acted the way he did I knew I wasn't that bad, I wasn't constantly drunk, I wasn't stealing, I wasn't crashing into cars over and over again and then driving away.

The Seizure

The end of the year was approaching, I had survived despite my best efforts at not surviving, and I had even made it relatively filled with joy for the sake of my son, Thanksgiving, Christmas went off without a hitch and were filled with smiles, laughs, and joy, and here we were on New Years Day journeying to the Sarah Anna to celebrate Russian New Year with the Russians, to play in the Sarah Anna, and as a mark of good faith I've decided not to drink today, something I haven't done in the last 9 months. But I figured let's end the year on a positive note and start the new year fresh. Playing in the Sarah Anna Anna proved to be an exciting and fresh adventure, my head was clear, my heart was filled with happiness, and Danny was having a great time. After we left the Sarah Anna Anna we drove back to my in-laws home to prepare for the evening's dinner and party with some of their close friends; I stayed true to my goal and hadn't drunk during the day, as the evening wore on I developed a headache, I couldn't stop staring at Igor who was drinking beer-I just wanted one, just a sip even, so I convinced him to let me have just a sip of his. It helped, the headache went away, I was less hot, but I needed more; a promise is a promise though so I persisted without more. I went to the kitchen after dressing to help his mom continue preparing food, the friends had arrived so as usual the women were in the kitchen cooking and the men were smoking cigarettes and drinking, Danny and another little girl were playing with toys in the family room.

Preparing Russian dishes were always a fun and interesting experience, something it's taken years to learn and be able to be helpful at making. My mother in law had just passed me a knife and cutting board to cut the sausages while her friend was setting the table, I went to begin cutting and the next thing I knew was waking up in the hospital. I thought I was cutting sausages, I didn't know how I ended up in the hospital, who was this man next to me, why were doctors and nurses looking at me? I had no memory of who Igor was, no memory of what had happened, no memory of coming to the hospital, I knew I was a mom but I couldn't remember my son's name. I was Britney Thomas, I was 24 years old, I was from Alabama. I wasn't married, I couldn't be married I was too young. Turns out I had had a seizure, a grand-mal seizure from detoxing from alcohol, I was released from the hospital on New Years eve night 45 minutes before midnight, we went back to the in-laws house, my memory was coming back, though I had no memory of falling on the floor and shaking, I had no memory of my father in law sticking a metal spoon in my mouth, I had no memory of the seizure. I was scared, if this is what happens when I stop drinking then surely I should continue drinking. I had only stopped because of Igor's ultimatum, I wanted to drink, but I wanted a baby, I wanted to pretend everything was fine; it wasn't. We finished out the night, I stayed sober, I ate little, and eventually, I fell asleep and thus ended the year of 2012. 2013 started out with possibilities, the possibility of moving from Washington state to California, the possibility of having a baby, the possibility of not drinking anymore. The first few weeks I spent going to doctors trying to figure out why I had a seizure, why I couldn't get pregnant, and researching places to live in Northern California. We were going to move to the San Francisco Bay Area, a chance to start fresh, no more drunken memories, beer hiding places everywhere, and it was a chance to get away from my family! After countless doctors appointments it was determined I had Polycystic ovary syndrome, and I had a random seizure based on my drinking history it was brought about because I stopped drinking suddenly, both diagnoses sent me on a spiral, my ovaries weren't cooperating, my body needed alcohol so I did what any sane person would do and I started drinking again. I started out slow, I drank only in the evenings limiting myself to only 5 or 6 beers, but a week into the drinking, two weeks before our move date I was back to 8 to 12 beers a night, sometimes during the day, I blamed it on the stress but in reality the knowledge that maybe I couldn't stop drinking was setting in. I became Christian and began praying to a god, and God really, but since my family was Christian it was the easiest, "please God, let me get pregnant so I can stop drinking, please god if only I can stop drinking" I just needed a reason to stop, I wasn't a reason, my son wasn't a reason, marriage wasn't a reason, but I couldn't stop.

Danny and I can't a plane from Seattle to San Francisco the last week of January, I took a few pre-boarding drinks before climbing onto the plane, once we arrived in the bay area I would be around Igor and his father non stop so I knew I had to prepare myself for the time ahead. By the time we boarded the plane I was relaxed, Danny and I had an enjoyable flight and we landed in San Francisco excited for our new life, Igor and his dad had reached the hotel so Danie and I took a taxi there, we checked in, and Igor and his dad went to find parking for the Uhaul while Danny and I went to find a beer for mommy and check out our surroundings. After the beer, I found a nearby place for us all to eat dinner and by the time Igor and his dad returned my breath was free from the smell of beer and Danny was telling his dad and grandpa we had enjoyed sodas while waiting for them. We ate dinner at a Chinese place and made a plan for the next day we had a max of 6 days to find a place to live, we had decided on Sunnyvale, Mountain View, Redwood City, Santa Clara as potential areas to live, we found listings of potential houses and apartments and settled on a nine am start time. We found a place on the second day of searching, submitted applications for a three-bedroom apartment, they accepted dogs and cats, and crossed our fingers for approval. I had bad credit, bad decisions as an eighteen-year-old left me in debt and with no current income I had no way of paying it off, but between Igor and his father's incomes we were set and we were approved to move into our new apartment all 5 of us would share along with the giant dog and cat.

California living

February 2013 came along and I realized it had been weeks since I had a period, I knew I was unlikely to be pregnant based on the doctor's diagnosis but I had a flicker of hope even while sipping on the beer. My father in law had traveled back to Washington state to pack up his house and to begin the journey south with his wife, dog, and cat. I had settled into a routine of counting down till the Igor left for work than cracking open the first beer of the day, some days I would skip the afternoon beer and Danny and I would travel to local parks, beaches, and explore around us, on this day February 5, we went to the doctor and got a pregnancy test done, all of them over the counter tests showed negative but I wanted a blood test to be certain. After the doctor, Danny and I picked up more beer for me and then went and spent the afternoon walking near the ducks and playing at the playground while I sipped on a beer from my Starbucks cup.

The following day I found out I was pregnant, I was so scared, I drank a beer, as I was drinking the beer I realized what I was doing and panicked. I was so scared how could I drink a beer when I had just found out I was pregnant, I had a beer in my car hidden away from Igor, I knew what I had to do, but I was so afraid, I drank one more beer swore it was the last one, and then I broke the news to Igor that I was pregnant. He took the car away from me that night when he arrived home and realized I had drunk after finding out I was pregnant, he also told me if our kid came out retarded he would divorce me, and leave me and the kid homeless because he would not father a retarded child. I swore I would stop drinking, he laughed at me and told me we would see, he said to keep him posted as to if I was going to get an abortion, if the kid was retarded, or if it would be healthy.

I lived without my car for about a week during which I didn't drink, I got sober, I started walking daily with Danny, and I became a human again. I swore with each passing day that I would never drink again, I wanted to be a good mom, a healthy mom, I wanted the baby to be safe, happy, healthy, a good sibling for it's brother, I started watching what I ate, and once Igor's parents arrived I told them I was pregnant. I spent the first trimester of my pregnancy in fear, certain I had caused irrevocable harm to the baby, I made up for it by eating salmon, fish eggs, and a healthy balanced diet, no caffeine, and lots of fruits and vegetables, walking, and exploring with Danny. I went to the first ultrasound and was told the baby was healthy, it had a healthy heartbeat, and I was due to have a baby in October. The second trimester began and I began counting down till I could find the sex of the baby, I was convinced it would be a girl, and at the second ultrasound I was told I was having a girl but there was a problem. I never told anyone what the doctor told me that day, it was my burden to bear, but the doctor told me the baby girl was showing signs of having a rare but fatal condition where she would either die before birth, or would die shortly after delivery, her brain wasn't forming. I was shocked, saddened, and I knew the doctor had to be mistaken. I declined an abortion and I continued on I was over 20 weeks pregnant and I could feel her, I could feel her moving and there was no way I would end her life.

The rest of the pregnancy passed by quickly, third trimester ultrasound showed a perfectly developed and healthy baby girl. I was excited and in the first week of October I began having labor pains, it was deja vu of 5 years earlier, once again the Igor was drunk and I was in pain, I could have woken my in-laws but I refused to, I went outside at 2 am and began walking around in the dark counting the minutes between contractions, finally at 4 am I called the doctor's office and let them know what was going on, they advised me to wait an hour before coming in unless something dramatically changed, so I continued walking around, keeping track, at 5 am I went back inside the apartment and woke up the Igor, he was groggy but somewhat sober and agreed to drive me to the hospital. The birth of the baby girl we named Sarah Anna Anna was a long process but I won't bore you with details, needless to say, eventually she was born and after a few days in the hospital after having a c-section delivery we were released to go home.

Per my internal promise of no more drinking I didn't drink after giving birth to her, her, Danny, and I became a unit, at times it all seemed so much, how was I supposed to relax when I was constantly around either kids or in-laws, but I maintained, staying sober, not willing to admit I thought about alcohol all the time, or how much I missed it. I stayed sober throughout the end of 2013 and continued not drinking throughout much of 2014, we moved from our tiny 3 bedroom apartment into a 3 story 4 bedroom house giving us all much needed space, and life became a bit more manageable now that I had room to breathe. Danny was doing great in school as a kindergartener, and I had made a few mom friends and spent my days walking with Sarah

Anna Anna, spending time with mom's groups, or else sitting in my room-anything to avoid too much time talking to my in-laws.

Alcoholic in training

2015 came about and living with the in-laws was unraveling, Igor and his parents couldn't get along, he was angry and resentful at them, i was tired of having to share a kitchen with his mother and tired of having to share my kids with her on a daily basis, I could grudgingly admit I appreciated her help but I was just tired of the internal struggle that was growing stronger every single day. We had finally reached an agreement that at the end of our lease we were going to go our separate ways, no more living together, finally! I was so excited, I immediately began searching for places to live meanwhile Igor and his parents continued bickering. I was so tired of it and at the end of the day I decided to drink for the first time in over a year, I don't know why I did it. I was telling myself I was going to congratulate myself, I had started real estate courses to become a realtor, I was moving away from his parents, life was falling into place, but just like when I had stopped drinking-I lacked control of when to stop drinking, one glass of wine turned to a bottle and I ended up drunk. I panicked I couldn't breastfeed because my milk was tainted but what if Igor found out, so I put the baby in our bed and promptly fell asleep next to her, Igor woke me at midnight angry, Sarah Anna Anna had woken up hungry and I was snoring. He knew I was drunk but he wanted me to admit it-I refused, i told him to feed her some milk she was over 1 year old and old enough for regular milk, I was tired. I fell back to sleep and he waited until the morning to confront me, he reminded me of his ultimatums, I quickly assured him I was just stressed out because of his parents, and looking for houses, and finding a place to live. He let it go, but I knew it was just beginning, I had woken up my desire to drink.

We moved away from his parents both of us going our own ways, but not too far so that they could still have time with their grandbabies and life settled into a new routine. We moved into a neighborhood filled with families from India, where Danny quickly became the minority, and I was given an excuse I needed to complain and be miserable. Not that I needed one but I was happy to have one all the same, and within weeks I began drinking. I stopped breastfeeding as soon as I realized I was going to drink I knew I couldn't endanger my daughter's healthy by drinking and so I made the decision to drink and not breastfeed. The drinking started out slow, I would spend the day taking Danny to school, spending time with other families and their kids, letting Sarah Anna Anna interact with others, then in the evening I would prepare food and start drinking. I started drinking beer in the evenings, counting down the minutes until 5 pm, counting down until 4 pm, each week it became earlier, each week I drank more until by April I knew Sarah Anna Anna had to go to preschool so that I could have free time to myself to drink. I was studying to become a realtor so I justified her schooling, got her enrolled in a Montessori then I could drink until midday and sober up enough to drive the kids home from school, do homework, then drink again in the evenings. I began hiding beer everywhere, Igor knew I had started drinking again, so I started hiding the drinks in clothes, the washer, dryer, cabinets, diaper bags, purses, behind the couch, in the bathroom-the bathroom was the best place I would frequently go to use the bathroom and take a drink while in there. Drinking became my priority every moment I spent awake I spent thinking about when I could drink, driving the kids to school I counted down till the moment I dropped my daughter off at school so that I could drink. I loved my kids to bits but I loved drinking, drinking was the solution to all of my problems. I wasn't happy at home, I hated myself, I was the worst mom, my son was struggling in school, my daughter hates preschool, and I couldn't pass the California state Real estate exam even after 3 failures, so I drank more. Drinking alleviated the feeling; I studied harder, I pushed Danny's school to evaluate him for speech and learning disabilities, and I spent more time with Sarah Anna Anna, I was operating and numbing. I was pulling further away from Igor, our time was mainly spent with ultimatums, dislike, arguments, and disappointing conversations.

Suicidal Thinking Part 2

August 2015 arrived, I had been drinking consistently since April, every month my consumption was increasing, my tolerance levels were through the roof, I was spending most of the grocery money on beer, beer wasn't working so I was adding in vodka and or wine, going through a minimum of 15 beers a day with a few other drinks thrown in, the kids were spending days with the grandparents since it was summer and me trying to get myself out of my funk I signed up for a 5k for an inflatable racecourse. To this day I reflect back on my thinking, how could I possibly complete a 5-kilometer race when I couldn't go a few hours without a drink but it was another way of trying to get myself sober, however, it took without admitting that I had a problem, without admitting I needed help. Needless to say, the week before the race dawned and I got wasted and went on a binge drinking non stop for 3 days until I reached a point of yet another ultimatum, a hysterical argument between Igor and I and me feeling as though the only way to survive this world was to in fact die. I was suicidal, I was miserable, and I was convinced I was ruining my kids lives and they would be better off without their mother.

I drank beer after beer, I took shot after shot of vodka, I dropped the kids off with their grandparents and I locked myself inside the home with my alcohol, with every beer I drank I could feel nothing, it wasn't working, I was on beer 13,14, 15, 16, nothing was working, vodka shot, half a pint of vodka gone and I was still coherent, why wasn't I drank, numb, passed out? I was so frustrated, I was so sad, angry, upset, I just wanted it to end, I wanted to end the pain, end the frustration, end it all and so I decided to add some pills to my cocktail, if the alcohol wasn't enough adding in sleeping pills, anti-nausea pills, pain pills would surely do the trick. Sure enough within minutes I felt myself drifting off, the room was spinning, the floor was moving, I was upside down, I was high, the world suddenly wasn't so bad, so I called my mom who called Igor, who picked me up and drove me to the hospital as fast as he could. It was just like

2012 only 3 years later in California instead of Washington; they wouldn't listen to me, they didn't believe I wasn't suicidal, and told me I was stuck in the hospital for the next few days. I was being held against my will, I had lost my rights the moment I drank and used drugs to excess, to numb out, my blood alcohol content was more than double the limit, close to being triple the amount, I couldn't stand, I couldn't remember the last time I had ate food, my body was revolting all things, and I was given charcoal to reduce the effects, and was monitored closely. I kept threatening to walk out of the hospital so eventually they placed a security guard in front of the door to my room. My Igor had left as soon as they called me back and assured him I wouldn't die, he was angry at me and out of patience. So I laid in the hospital bed waiting for my alcohol to leave my system and be released, eventually they told me that I was going to be transferred to a different location, I asked to call my Igor but they wouldn't let me. I was handcuffed to the bed, and wheeled out to a waiting ambulance. The ambulance transferred me to Oakland, into a scary neighborhood, I was unloaded to a mental hospital that was in charge of me for the next 72 hours, they would determine if I would be held longer, I had to behave my life, my freedom was at stake. I was weak and couldn't walk so they brought me to the intake. I was checked in, asked a million questions most of which were differently phrased but the same questions, why had I tried to kill myself?

The next 3 days of my life proved to be a scary experience, living in a mental hospital meant no locked doors, no shut doors, the bathrooms gave some privacy but at any time a nurse could walk in to check on you. Taking a shower meant checking out a towel from the nurse, you weren't allowed shoe strings, normal bras were not allowed, socks were monitored, and often people came in like me, with no extra clothes, we didn't plan to go to the mental hospital. I had to ask for clean clothes, a toothbrush, a comb, and everything else. I was escorted to the shower and had to have help to take it, I hadn't eaten in more than 4.5 days, I only drank the minimum amount of water, my body was weak, they ordered me to take a shower and eat food. My first encounter with food went horribly, as soon as I ate it was coming back out of my body in every way imaginable. The next day dawned bright and early every hour there was a therapy to attend and if I wanted out I was going to have to participate; so I went to codependent therapy, alcoholics therapy, coping skills, music therapy, art therapy, physical activity, I ate as was required of me, I listened, I shared, I told them I was an alcoholic, and at the end of the day I got to meet the shrink, or as he preferred to be called the psychiatrist. He told me I was depressed and I needed to take medicine, I smiled, nodded, and told him I wasn't going to take meds, I would do therapy but I didn't need medicine. He told me he would visit me the next day and to think on it. The next day and day after went by incredibly slowly, I got energy, I ate, I grew stronger, I got a visitor, and talked to the kids, I stayed busy, I admitted over and over my drinking problem, I sang songs, and talked to fellow hospital guests. I was going to be released finally, I signed the release forms and I was picked up by Igor, he told me he was sorry he could finally understand that I was sick. We made an appointment for me to go to an Intensive Outpatient Rehab center a few days after leaving the hospital, I was nervous and apprehensive, they told me to come ready to pee and if I had drugs or alcohol in my system then I wouldn't be able to do the program.

I went to the IOP Rehab a few days later and knew immediately I wasn't going to do it, I had finally passed my Real Estate exam for California, my career was about to take off, I was fine, the mental hospital had put things into perspective, I wasn't an alcoholic, I just needed to stop drinking so much. I could do that, no problem! So I declined to attend and went back home, I stayed dry from alcohol for a few weeks and gradually I started drinking again, just one or two beers here or there, a few more a few days later, a small amount, controlling it wasn't so hard! But something I know now that I didn't know then is, is that it's exhausting trying to control your alcohol.

By October I was back to drinking just like I had before the stent to the mental hospital, albeit I was trying to hide it better. I stopped sleeping next to Igor altogether, it wasn't like we talked or had anything to say to each other, I blamed him for my drinking, and he hated me for my drinking amongst other things. So I slept in the kid's room often falling asleep with a beer in my hand, waking up at 1 or 2 am finishing the beer or 2 and going back to sleep. November came and I was supposed to attend a real estate seminar, however I chose to get wasted a few days beforehand and got my car and phone taken away, got left home while Igor went out to celebrate his birthday along with his friends, and so I took it as another opportunity to get wasted, the kids were with their grandparents again. That night as I was chugging away beer after beer and crying in the dark I made myself a promise to stop drinking, I was scared, I couldn't stop, and even though I hated my life, I hated my Igor, I hated

California, I loved my kids, and I was wasting my time with them. Sarah Anna Anna was two years old, Danny was seven years old, Danny was going to remember me this way, I didn't want that! I spent the night in a drunken haze messaging a few friends who had stopped drinking, I searched Facebook for ways to stop drinking and joined a few online groups, I saw person after person mention how many days they hadn't drunk alcohol in, it seemed so foreign! I had so many questions but decided to just keep quiet, read their stories and posts and see if they were liars.

December had arrived, I had survived Thanksgiving with only two beers drank, I was positive again, I was trying the sober thing. I would drink one day and stay sober another day, I kept relapsing, but I had faith and hope. I had to do this thing. I had proven my willingness to try and be sober so the Igor kindly agreed to take me with him to his company holiday party, it was to be held on a yacht that would cruise us around the San Francisco Bay. I was so excited to be included in something, but I was so nervous! I was going to be the designated driver, we drove to the city with no issues, the party itself was quiet, people were laughing and drinking, having a great time, why could they drink so amazingly? Why wasn't I like that! Look they could drink, so could I! The Igor got wasted, I half drug him, half carried him back from the boat to the car, I endured his slurs as he informed me how a useless drunk I was, how there were so many beautiful women he worked with, I listened and filed away every word he said, I wrestled him for the keys when he tried to drive. And eventually we were on our way home from his party, I was counting down till we were home. I was a loser and for losers there is only one way to cure the pain. I was going to drink and this time I didn't care, I wasn't going to hide it, I wasn't going to stop it. I went home got him in bed, and I started drinking, the next day he went to get the kids and I stayed home to drink more. I kept drinking pausing only to get the kids ready for bed. I passed out eventually woke the next morning, dropped the kids at school and drank again, I drank into the afternoons asking the Igor to pick up the kids. I drank, I drank, and I drank some more, I drank from December 6 until December 9 when Igor came home from work I was passed out on the floor.

And then there was Rock bottom

I woke up from my drunken stupor to being rushed to the hospital, Igor had told the paramedics I was unresponsive and he thought I was dying or dead. So there I was being rushed to the hospital though there was nothing wrong with me. I was so angry! Once I reached the hospital I yelled at them to release me, it wasn't their fault but there was no one else to be angry with aside from myself. Eventually, they released me after I was considered legally safe to be released, and I went home, found my beer and continued drinking. I drank all night, the kids had been brought to his parents house, and I woke up the next day on the floor, Igor had left for work. I decided something needed to change so I drank a morning beer and went to attend my first Alcoholics Anonymous meeting. I arrived there and my first thoughts were simply that I was nothing like these people. I drank a beer in the car while waiting for the meeting to start and 5 minutes beforehand I walked inside. They were so welcoming that it made me sick, or it could have been the beer I had just drunk at 830 in the morning. I sat through the entire meeting listening to slogan after slogan, drunk after drinking sharing their experiences, strength, and hope, I got a pamphlet filled with phone numbers of who to call if I felt like drinking, and I heard the final piece of advice- alcohol will never taste the same after you attend an AA meeting. I left the meeting in a huff, straight to the car, straight to the liquor store, and straight to a park to drink the beer, it wasn't working! Maybe that A person was onto something.

That night Igor came home after work, his mood was worse than it normally was, he knew I was drinking, he had sent me an email earlier in the day, so I read it. I was upset, I was angry, I was hurt, I had a solution. I told him I was done drinking, I begged him not to leave me, his email told me he was going to divorce me, he was going to set up housing for the kids and I, but he was done. He told me face to face he meant his email, I started crying, begging, and finally I told him okay, I just want to go to an AA meeting- he grudgingly said fine about watching the kids, I grabbed a bottle of champagne-the last of the alcohol, a bottle of Dom perignon my dad had given me from the year of my birth 1988, and I left the house. It was December 11, 2015, at 7 pm, there was an AA meeting at 730pm, and it was raining, I popped the top of the champagne and started drinking it. I left the apartments and started driving around, at some point during the 3rd or 4th chug of champagne I blacked out. I don't know how long I was driving for, I don't know where I drove too, I drove in circles, and at some point started calling Igor to find me. I was drunk, I was scared, I wanted help.

Igor eventually found me, I had hit something and knocked the bumper off the car, I had peed in the seat, I was a mess. I was drunk and in between blackouts, he caught me in a good moment and moved me into his car with the children, then he called the cops on me. He went and sat on the curb and eventually the cops arrived, I had passed out in the driver's seat of Igor's car with the kids sitting confusedly in the back seat. The cops woke me up, tweedle dee and tweedle dum; cop one was the aggressor, he right away started asking me questions, threatening me, he upset me, I told him to leave me alone and go talk to my asshole Igor. Cop 2 stayed and spoke to me, he asked me what I wanted to do with my life ,he asked me what message I wanted to send to my kids, he asked me what I was doing the driving, I stared at him shocked. He was right, oh but here came the first cop, he was back threatening me, demanding of me to get out of the car, I asked him to please be nice for the sake of my kids, I had never driven like this with them in the car, the keys were not even in the car, I loved my kids more than anything. He finally heard me, he gave me a choice, was I going to jail or to the hospital, I told him to fuck off, he went back to again talk to the Igor who had snitched on me. Cop 2 looked at me, he told me to think clearly, wouldn't I rather sober up, get help, be a good mom, there is nothing wrong with admitting I have a drinking problem and going to the hospital, if I love my kids that's what I should do, otherwise they would see mom getting arrested. I thought it over for a moment and agreed, I would go to the hospital. I told my kids bye and how much I loved them and walked to the waiting ambulance for my final ride to the hospital.

Once at the hospital I realized what was going on, I panicked, there was no way I was going back to the mental hospital ever again, I screamed and told them over and over that I wasn't suicidal, I didn't want to die, I would never drink again but to release me immediately. They didn't listen, my alcohol content was over 3 times the legal limit, they didn't understand how I was still conscious, I had alcohol poisoning, I was dehydrated, I was functioning like an alcoholic, my body was going into detox and it was only 2 hours since my last drink, if I didn't let them help me I could have a seizure, I could die, I needed to let them help me. I spit on nurses, I screamed at the security guard, the doctors threatened me with the police if I didn't let them check me out, I finally quieted down enough to tell them I've had a seizure before. They asked me to take anti seizure medicine, I agreed to take half if the assured me I wasn't going to a mental hospital. They agreed on the condition I settle down, stop fighting, screaming, and take the medicine and agree to talk to a psychiatrist in the morning. I agreed.

The next day I woke up rested, hungover, and slightly confused, the pill they had given me knocked me out the night before, my alcohol was approaching the normal levels, and they were pumping me full of water, I was stabilized but I wasn't out of the woods completely yet. I still had another 48 hours of true detoxing before I would be cleared from having seizures, delirium tremens, major dehydration, I also had the shakes, I couldn't stop sweating, my head was throbbing, and I was nauseous. Alcohol was needed but I couldn't have it, I wanted to be sober, I knew I was approaching divorce, my life was going to change and I needed to face it. The psychiatrist came to speak with me, he told me about alcoholism, how some consider it a disease-possibly it was for me, a disease or a severe allergy I didn't have the mechanism of stopping at any point if I drank I would die. I listened intently to the doctor only bringing out the minimal amount of a smartass than I was. After the doctor visited me, I set up a follow up appointment with a psychiatrist in his office for a few days later and eventually the Igor came to pick me up. I was informed he was taking me home, he had brought the car home, I needed to clean it, and the kids were staying with his parents for the next few days, he didn't care if I drank or not but he didn't want to talk to me. I just nodded mutely, I accepted this, I knew he had made up his mind and I was just tired. I was dropped off at home, I knew when AA meetings were so I humbled myself and drove myself to a meeting. I walked in and I was welcomed back, some made a few jokes about me not smelling like beer today and it made me realize I hadn't fooled anyone yesterday. These people knew the signs better than I did because they were all sober and willing to admit their problems, I listened that day to their shares, to their stories. I understood what they were talking about, the inability to not drink, the insanity of feeling lonely, angry, lost, confused, happy, sad, everything in between and needing to numb it with alcohol. Some stories were so extreme of people drinking mouthwash and in my head I would compare myself only to realize that that could easily be me, give me a week, a month and I too would drink mouthwash, rubbing alcohol, anything to feel numb. I didn't want that. I wanted to be alive. I wanted to be a mom. I stayed after the meeting to talk to the ladies of the group, I was afraid to go home, I didn't want to be alone, I was scared I would drink, I realized there was another meeting, and a meeting after that, so my plan for the day was created, I would sit in meeting after meeting until there were no more meetings that day. I listened to share after share, story after store, I felt scared, but at the end of the night I realized I hadn't drank alcohol in over 24 hours. I could do this! So I went home, I started writing posts in the groups online I had joined, there were people awake in Australia and two kind ladies took mercy on me and talked to me that night until I finally fell asleep. Those two ladies were so kind and reassuring me, they hadn't been sober for too long, but they were sober, they were moms, and they were doing this life thing.

The next day I went back to a meeting, and stayed in meetings all day, my kids had spoken to me in the morning and were asking when they could come home, if mommy was feeling better; I reassured them I was getting better but they couldn't come home yet. I hadn't heard from their dad, he was ignoring my texts and not coming home. I focused on myself, I listened at meetings until I finally heard a lady share, she had what I wanted, to be strong, independent, sober, dignified. I asked her to be my sponsor and thankfully she said yes, and so my first relationship in sobriety began. I shared with her my drinking styles, the last two months were the worse when I was drinking 30 something beers a night plus vodka or wine, I was passing out, missing out on life, going to the hospital countless times, and generally ruining my life and health. I was suicidal but I didn't want to die, and all i wanted was to be a mom to my two beautiful kids, I was going to get divorced and I helping some clients close on their house. I was barely functioning and I've tried everything in my power to pretty much end my life, but I need help, I don't want to drink.

With the help of meetings and my sponsor I stayed sober one day, two days, three days, I was going to meetings two to three days a week, on the fourth day of sobriety the Igor returned home, he said he wanted to stay with me, he was proud I was attending meetings, he could tell I was sober, he wanted to be able to say he had supported me in my darkest hour. I didn't care, I was just happy to not get divorced, I was happy to have my kids back, and so a few weeks passed and we went on our first vacation to Lake Tahoe, he drank while we were there and my first test was passed, I didn't drink, I stayed sober, and I was so happy and proud of myself. We returned in time to celebrate the New Year with his parents, again I was tested when they all drank whiskey and champagne and I realized this was going to be my life, he was going to drink even if it made it hard for me so I accepted it, I wasn't going to let him win. I was going to stay sober no matter what. I was posting throughout the day in online groups, texting my sponsor, and regularly attending meetings, my sobriety date was December 11, and I am proud of every day that I was accumulating.

I celebrated my first month of sobriety by making an appointment to get a new tattoo, I wanted something big that would be a constant reminder of all that I had accomplished, the tattoo I was getting was a combination of my kids, a pixelated heart in honor of my son and his love for minecraft and a snowflake for my daughter and her name Sarah Anna Anna. The tattoo process was over in a few hours and to this day it's one of my most favorite tattoos. The next few months passed by sometimes quickly sometimes slowly, I began working the 12 steps of AA with my sponsor, and I spent many weekends crying hysterically, I wasn't what my Igor wanted me to be, so what I had sold a house and made commission, so what I was sober, I still wasn't skinny enough, I was fat, I wasn't smart enough, why didn't I sell more houses, I wasn't good enough, I wasn't Russian, I couldn't keep a house clean, I couldn't cook. I was never good enough but the steps were teaching me that it didn't matter-what matter was what I felt for myself. I had to love myself and not seek love from outside myself, it could compliment me but I couldn't rely on it. He was sick, he was mean, he was cruel, but I could either accept him or I had to move on, but first I needed to wait till one year sober before making any large decisions. I spent my first 6 months in tears every weekend and most of the week, everything I did was wrong, but at least I was sober, we had made an agreement to not have alcohol in our house and he stuck with his agreement for the first 5 months until he decided to host a borscht party for his friends at our home. They brought beer and vodka, and I made borscht, I was miserable but as he pointed out, he made the money, he made the decisions, and he paid the rent, I did nothing.

I caught a break at 7 months sober, I had lost some weight, I was deemed acceptable to present to the public in Igor's company, and he invited me to go to the car races with him. I was excited I loved riding in his car while he was acting crazy and driving fast. We drove down south from Northern California to Southern California with his friend and him, the races were amazing and allowed us both to get an adrenaline rush especially as the first race he lost the brakes on his car and had to do a lot of downshifting to control his speed, it was exciting and I loved it, it was another form of a high and I didn't want it to stop. We spent the day at the races and in the evening we continued our drive south to Orange County California where he was going to be interviewed for a position within a small company. I made plans to meet up with a woman I had met through an online group-we had been talking consistently for a few months, I was nervous to meet her but I was excited to meet her as well. So that night the Igor went to his interview and I went out alone to eat by myself, I went to bed early so that I could wake up super early to meet my new friend while he slept in, he had drunk a few glasses of whiskey the night before and was snoring in bed. I was so happy to escape the smell of him, I met her at a Starbucks and we instantly clicked, she was 2 months soberer than I was, she was a mom, and I knew we were destined to be great friends. I told her about the interview and she told me about where she lives and the benefits, I was hopeful, I hugged her bye and told her I would press to move down here, the beach, weather, and she was all huge positives. I went back to the hotel and woke up the Igor, we began our drive back to northern California, stopping in Los Angeles so that he could buy a giant bong, along the way, and once back I begged him to take the job no matter what. He agreed but the snag was school down there started 2 weeks before school up north, I wanted Danny to begin on time, so we arranged for kids and I to move south by ourselves, it was the happiest moment in my life up to that moment.

Life in Socal

The kids and I loaded up the prius and began our journey south on an early morning in August, we were loaded up and excited for our adventure, we were stress free and filled with smiles. We were moving to Aliso Veijo the same city as my new friend, and we were going to be living alone for 3 months, Danny started 3rd grade and I had switched real estate brokerages and was looking for a new Montessori preschool for Sarah Anna Anna to attend.

The three months flew by, every morning the kids went to school, after drop off I would go to the work office or I would go to AA meetings, I made acquaintances, I spent as much time with my new friend discussing our lives, and having walks near the beach, I spent free time with the kids going to Legoland, disneyland, the beach, cooking dinner and settling into a routine. The Igor came to visit twice, showing off, pretending to be the father of the year and with every visit it was nice but more nice when it came to an end. After the second visit he left to go finish packing our stuff up in northern california; while packing he found vitamins and proceeded to get into an argument with me, why was I taking prenatal vitamins, I had lied about getting my tubes tied, was that it? Was I pregnant, he didn't want more children. I started crying, I took the vitamins because they were high in B vitamins and it was easier than taking a mixture of vitamins. He didn't believe me, I was reduced back to being a liar, a loser. He hated me, I hated him, I was so tired of his treatment of me. I cried to my friend who told me to stay strong, I didn't need him, he doesn't treat me good, I'm young and I can do better.

A month later the Igor moved south, we found a house that we would move into, it had 7 bedrooms and 8 bathrooms, a swimming pool, a huge kitchen, and most importantly enough room for his parents to move in with us. He had forgotten why it hadn't worked the first time, I was in no position to argue, I was 2 months shy of 1 year sober, I had a program I worked, I was solid in my recovery, he was smoking weed, and it was happening because once again I didn't make money, I was a mom, and that's it, so financially I was not entitled to an opinion. We celebrated Halloween together with the kids by taking them trick or treating, I registered Danny the next day for his new school and we moved into our gigantic house. We began preparing to host Igor's 30th birthday which he wanted to be a big bash at our new house, his parents would drive down to attend, along with his friends, and god parents.

Igor's 30th birthday bash was a big hit, I invited my friend and she was greeted at the door by my father in law thrusting a bottle of vodka in her face, I was so mad, I told them not to but as usual just like his son he ignored me, he thought it was funny. My Igor got drunk and tore his Achilles tendon while jumping into the pool, overall his 30th turned out to be a memorable experience for everyone. I had survived a big drunken Russian party. A few weeks later we celebrated my first sober Thanksgiving which thankfully was a quiet affair with only a few guests, I overcooked the turkey and thankfully no one complained except for Igor. He was often critical, I was constantly on edge from Thanksgiving until Christmas I felt like he was doing everything he could to try and get me to drink, I was on an emotional roller coaster and longed for the days of him living away from me.

December 11, 2016 marked one year sober, I was so excited and happy, my friend treated me to a birthday dinner which was amazing and at home Igor had forgotten what the day was until he noticed I had received gifts from a few friends. He decided to take me and his friend and the kids out for sushi, he cheered me by drinking beer with his friends, they both found it hilarious to drink on my sober birthday. I was so angry, they were mocking me-again-I was fed up but I just smiled and got through it. I started attending a new meeting with my friend and got to pick up my one year chip from it. I was happy, I knew I would make it my new home group and hopefully get a sponsor, I had lost interest in meetings for a while but was missing them.

The new year had came, I had survived my first year of sobriety, my first sober thanksgiving, my second sober CHristmas and New Years, and here I was in 2017 and it was going to be a great year, I knew how to be sober now and I could survive anything. The new year started off with my grandmother dying, I made arrangements to fly to Washington alone for her funeral-another big test for sobriety, facing my brothers, and family while maintaining sobriety. I was scared and nervous but I wasn't willing to miss her funeral. I landed in Washington with a plan, I told my brothers not to talk to me, I spent time with a cousin, and saw my Aunts, and Uncles, I visited, and attended a few meetings. I worked my program and at the end of the weekend I was sober and stronger. I flew back to California declining the free beer and free wine and once back made plans to have knee surgery to repair a torn ACL in March. I wanted to have a healthy body, a healthy mind, and now was a great time as I had help from my in-laws.

March 7, 2017 I went to have knee surgery, surgery was scheduled for 7 am which meant arriving by 6 am, Igor had accompanied me to the surgery center, right after they had inserted the IV into my arm my Igor decided that was the moment to inform me he was struggling with the fact that I hadn't had an abortion, he knows Danny is his, he has the DNA tests to prove it but I had trapped him in marriage. I was wheeled back to surgery after that, crying silently, and a part of me hoping I didn't wake up. It seemed my past was never going to allow me to escape. I was forever in hell. I woke up from surgery to see that I had indeed survived it, I was sore and in pain but the Igor's mood had improved, I knew it wasn't over yet, but I let it go, I was nauseous and started throwing up within hours after having surgery. In response to his mood, in response to my feeling ill the Igor decided that that was the day to get me a replacement car, the other car's lease was approaching the end anyways and he had found a good deal. I went with him and saw the car, I tried to be grateful but I was miserable, I couldn't stop throwing up and shortly after he drove me home thankfully.

A few weeks after having knee surgery the conversation came back to abortions and marriage entrapment, he was so angry and knew I had trapped him, he wouldn't listen to reason and I was out of patience, I had a sponsor but I couldnt' call her, this guy was venting on me again, I was sick of it. I was always the target, the scapegoat, I loaded the kids up in the new car, and me in a full leg brace and leg locked into a stiff position left the house-I told his parents they needed to deal with their son and I turned off my phone and left. The kids and I drove 2 hours south to San Diego, I needed a break, i couldn't deal anymore and there was no way I was ruining my life for this guy, not anymore. Eventually kids and I went back home, I made an appointment with a divorce lawyer for the next day and went. THe lawyer told me straight out if I didn't brave up I would never divorce, I was scared, no income, no job, I didn't feel like I had any choice but to stay.

Sober Living

The rest of 2017 passed by slowly, I stayed sober, life with the Igor was one argument after another, he was forever angry and resentful at me, and by the end of the summer things were at their worst. I was depressed and I was struggling to pull myself out of the funk, we had moved houses again, his parents were going to move back to the Bay area and we moved to a smaller home. He was less stressed since he know longer had to pay for everyone and I quit my short term part time job to go back to being a full time stay at home mom again, I hated being a realtor so I didn't even both with it anymore. For Labor day he decided we were going to go to Hawaii, just the two of us, it would be our first ever vacation just us two and I was excited to go. We were going to Maui, beautiful water, warm weather, beautiful beaches, and lots of time together, surely this was what our relationship needed, a chance for us to spend time together just us two, sober. Sadly what is often thought of as amazing for most people often doesn't happen that way in real life, Maui was beautiful, the water warm and gorgeous, snorkeling was magical, but after the first half day of snorkeling the Igor was done, he was mad that I forced him to go to Maui, I forced him to not play games, I took time away from his precious free time. I was hysterical, I thought we were having a romantic trip, instead once again I was an evil person, I took the rental car and drove to the village to spend the day by myself, I went to starbucks, I went shopping, I ate, and eventually I drove back to our resort, he was playing video games and ignoring me. I went for a walk on the beach at sunset and at dinner by myself, I sat in the sand and stared at the stars. Hawaii was beautiful and one of the best places I had ever been and I was grateful to have been able to come, I steeled myself for the forthcoming argument and slowly walked back to the room to go to sleep; tomorrow was a new day.

The next day in Hawaii the Igor woke up in a new mood- he was going to make the best of it, so we drove on the road to Hilo, I tried to stay in the moment, I couldn't let yesterday ruin today, it was there under the surface in the fake smiles and overly kind gestures, but I focused on hiking to waterfalls, viewing the sights, experiencing the drive which was a windy road at times only dirt. The Igor drove fast and at times the drive was filled with fear, other times it was just laughter as we cruised over bumps, it didn't matter the company what mattered was the beauty outside. 8 hours after beginning our drive around Maui we returned to our room to change and go out to dinner, the next day we were going to be leaving, I felt angry, resentful, but I also knew better than to show any of it, I had to remain grateful otherwise I would never again be allowed to go on a trip. Sobriety had taught me at times that it was best to fake things until you could have privacy to react alone. That was my mantra when it came to my marriage, to keep my head low, to accept everything thrown at me, to accept that I'm just the wife-I make no money, I serve no purpose except to mother kids, and nowadays I don't drink. It was sad, depressing, and exhausting living like this and at times, especially on 6 hour flights I hated myself for putting up with it, I spent the flight home asking myself why I deserve this, why was I punishing myself? Didn't I deserve respect, kindness, love, why was I inflicting pain on myself for my past? For the fact I had a baby, and another baby, what was the message I wanted my kids to see? But I had no answers aside from surviving, I had no income, I had little self esteem, little self worth, and I was convinced this is all I deserved, I would never find anyone to love me because half the time I couldn't love myself. Sobriety had given me the gift and desire to live, but I was still struggling with the concept of deserving things, of deserving happiness, kindness, love. Coming back from Hawaii, I was relaunched into the world of parenting, taking kids to school, going to PTA meetings, listening to moms and parents talk about wine brunches, wine nights out, and the many things they did for fun away from their kids, when I wasn't involved in school activities I was attending AA meetings, hanging out with my closest friend, and plotting our next sober meetup to hang out with people like us who didn't drink. We fell into a routine of life, counting down the days till my friend reached her 3rd sober birthday, counting down to my daughter's birthday. Life was simple as long as I didn't dig too deep into personal relations with the Igor life was fine, but it just kept popping up. Every three weeks my friend and I would meet at starbucks and over coffee and tea discuss our relationships, the constant theme for both of us being why am I staying in a relationship, I'm young, pretty, and the kids are young, and deserve a happy mom. I spend too much time miserable, crying, and hating my life, I was sober so the least I could do is treat myself better; my dilemma was the unknown, what would life be like single, I would never find happiness, love, or someone again, Igor would go off and be happy and I would be all alone. It was an excuse, fear, but it was so real that I couldn't see any alternatives, and when I wasn't letting fear stand in my way I was using the kids as a reason to stay. The rest of 2017 and going into 2018 passed by in a trend of having a few weeks of common rest, getting along, followed by arguments, resentments overflowing, and tears flowing. Sarah Anna Anna's birthday, Thanksgiving, and Christmas were made happy by my taking momentous efforts to ensure the kids had great memories, I spent the fall and winter exhausted, I celebrated my 2nd sober birthday, and the day after Christmas the kids were driven up to stay with their grandparents for a few weeks during winter break. Those few weeks allowed me to sleep, to watch movies, and to have a relatively happy new years eve with the Igor it consisted of watching the entire Lord of the Rings series through the night. It was fun, but the following day the bubble was broken when I reminded him I was driving 16 hours alone to get the kids, he refused to go, he refused to see his parents, and I was the one who had chosen this so I had to do it. I happily drove and got the kids arriving back home with a speeding ticket.

Recovering out Loud

January 2018 went by followed by February 2018, my recovery was my focus as well as the kids, taking them to school, coming home working on homework. Mid February Danny caught a cold that led to the loudest cough I've ever heard, I took him to doctor after doctor searching for the reason for his cough only to be told it would pass or he was faking it. I was so exhausted by March that I didn't know what to do. My birthday was approaching, Danny's cough had improved only to come back worse than before, but I was doing the best I could and following doctor's advice. A few days before my birthday the Igor decided we were going to fly to San Francisco to meet with his friends, at first he was going to go alone before I reminded him it was my birthday, he was mad, he didn't want me to go, but I guilt tripped him until he finally agreed. So the day before my birthday kids, Igor, and I boarded the plane, Igor was excited and also angry, one of his friends was going to meet us at the airport to pick us up and bring us to our hotel. As we were getting off the plane in Oakland the pilot's offered to let the kids view the cockpit and the kids were so excited so I paused and let them see, only to get off the plane to an angry guy staring at me, he was furious that I had taken the time to stop, how dare I? I was confused and hurt but I kept my mouth closed and just walked mutely with him so that I didn't create a scene.

We were driven to our hotel where as soon as we arrived Igor left to go hang out with his friends and the kids and I went to bed. Igor stayed out most of the night arriving back early in the morning, a few short hours later the kids were up and ready to begin the day, they wished me a happy birthday, and so as to not bother Igor we left the room to go for a walk. We were near the tenderloin, so I was careful to avoid going too far so as to not expose the kids to the sad sights, we stumbled upon a coffee shop and ended up meeting the friends on coincidence at the same time, I called Igor and woke him up, he was angry, grumpy, but he remembered we were here to visit with his friends from Washington state so he agreed to meet us there. He showed up eventually and we all had breakfast, the friend's wife shared she was pregnant with her second baby so we celebrated her. We all made plans to go back to change clothes and then spend the day in San Francisco, going to the tallest point in the city, followed by fisherman's wharf, by that time it was mid afternoon and the guy's were ready to leave to play video games. I was given a gift of cash and told to have a good birthday, before Igor left to do his own thing; his dad was going to come pick up the kids, and so I would spend a few hours with the friend's wife before having the night to myself. Happy Birthday to me. I booked myself a ticket to an Improv comedy show, on the way the uber driver complimented me on how pretty I looked and offered to escort me to the show, I was terrified and tried to call Igor only to have my call rejected. I was sad but I refused to let my birthday just pass by like any other day, so I went to the show, I smiled, and laughed, and afterwards I took myself to a lone birthday dinner at a local sushi restaurant.

The next day, I woke up to Igor stumbling into the room, he was drunk, hungover, and not in the mood to speak to me, he hadn't come home the night before, though his friend had managed to. I was upset, but I knew it was pointless, I was not in the mood to be reminded how he generously took me to San Francisco for my birthday though he didn't spend it with me except for a few hours during which he acted like a jerk majority of the time. So I just smiled and went downstairs to talk to the friends, I agreed to hang out with them for a while before I would go on my own, the kids were staying with the grandparents until we would head to the airport later in the night. Midday Igor said goodbye to his friends before he went to spend the day with some other friends and go to the Russian Sauna, at first he was going to invite me to the bbq, but at some point he changed his mind, so I walked from midtown to Chinatown, from Chinatown to Little Italy, from there I walked to Pier 39, and eventually I walked back up the hills to our hotel, it was lonely, it was enjoyable, and I walked about 9 miles that day up and down hills, I spent the time thinking, trying to not feel pity for myself, and growing angrier by the minute, I deserved better than this!

After the trip to San Francisco things evened out; I figured out what was wrong with Danny And why he was coughing-he had

WHooping Cough and was banned from going to school until he was declared disease free. He missed over two months of school and during that time I spent weeks arguing with his school getting him a private tutor, asking them to launch an investigation how my vaccinated son had caught a disease, I got him tested for Autism, and by May he was declared disease free and labeled as a high functioning autism. I was happy to have some answers as to why he struggled in school, why he refused to look people in the eye, and mostly just happy that his school would be more understanding about him and stop punishing him for being the way he was. I talked to him about being labeled and suggested he never let anyone use it against him-it was a gift, and he could embrace the gift or be angry, it was his choice, ultimately though, he is who he is, Autistic, not autistic didn't change him. After finding out about Danny's diagnosis I had too much free time and conquering a fear I finally launched a group for people seeking recovery, I worked harder on my podcast, and I started working on becoming a Recovery Coach. I wanted to have an income, I wanted my own business, I wanted to be able to work while being a full time mom, I invested my time, I interviewed people for my podcast, and I put myself out there. After launching my group for alcoholics, drinkers, drug addicts, addicts, people seeking a life without drugs or alcohol I planned my first majore meetup in Atlanta, Georgia, it was an excuse to escape home, I was excited to get away from my life for just a weekend and focus on myself. I worked hard on launching my group in all aspects, hosting weekly, sometimes twice a week online meetings, engaging the group in topics, and getting people excited about life. I may have been dying on the inside in regards to my relationship but I was making the best effort, I kept trying to be a better wife, a better human, I kept trying to keep a cleaner house, create fancier dinners, I dived into exercise since I was perpetually always to fat, my stomach to flabby, my thighs to large. I wanted to be perfect though I knew perfection was unachievable. I kept trying to be whatever Igor wanted, diving into people pleasing, while daily reminding myself I shouldn't. July finally arrived and I flew off to Atlanta leaving the kids in the care of their grandmother. I had a full weekend planned starting off with a new tattoo on my ankle of a lotus flower-because I too was blooming from the mud, followed by lunches, dinners, and a trip to the Coca Cola Factory, it was the first time I had been in Atlanta since I was a kid, and it was just as I had remembered it. Southern food, southern charm, humidity, kindness, and thunderstorms, I felt at home, at peace, I laughed non stop, smiled continuously, and dove into the history of the area, completing the trip with hike to a local waterfall. It was a beautiful trip and I was elated as I returned home to California to be told that I should once again be grateful for the privilege; reality had returned with a vengeance so I in turn sought a way to numb myself without numbing my headspace, I picked up exercise.

August and September I exercised like an obsessed woman, I was obsessed, I wanted to lose weight, I wanted to be perfect,I didn't know what perfect would look like but I just kept focusing on exercising. I had a major sober even coming up in September and I planned to look fabulous. I exercised every day for two hours, I used weights, I threw myself into exercise classes and when I wasn't at the gym I was walking with the kids places, going to the beach, and embracing life. By the time mid September arrived I was happier with the way I was looking, my thighs weren't perfect, I didn't have 6 pack abs, but I felt healthier, so away I went for a long weekend in Los Angeles, I was meeting up with friends from my group on a Thursday and Friday, they had flown in from Scotland, Australia, the Northeast US, Pacifici Northwest, and Idaho, we met in Venice beach, walked, laughed, talked, went to dinner, and the next day we went to Rodeo Drive in Beverly Hills for the day. By the end of the day I was filled with happiness and excitement to attend the She Recovers conference with over 500 women in recovery. She recovers was a beautiful weekend, my friend and I shared a room, we spent the weekend waking up early, going to bed late, we hung out with women from around the world, we went to a late dinner, and shared clothes, we laughed and had a good time. The Saturday night was the big gala and we put our fancy dresses on and went to hear speakers share their experiences, strength, and hope, hearing amazing women share their stories were inspiring and empowering. After the gala some friends and I went in our party dresses and jumped in the pool. That weekend was a taste of what life was like when I wasn't stressed out about an Igor who treated me poorly, here I was being empowered, being encouraged to be me, these women accept me as I was, loud, friendly, childish, wild.

After She Recovers was finished I went back home to the world of being a quiet wife and a mom, I was filled with excitement and happiness, I knew what I wanted from life, I kept going to the gym daily, kept working on my body while plotting my next big trip to Rhode Island to attend a recovery concert. I had heard about the concert while attending She Recovers and knew I had to go; I wanted to hear Macklemore sing live, and I wanted away from my Igor. I love my kids, but I hated being home, I felt trapped, I felt horrible, so I convinced him to book me a red eye ticket and I left the last weekend in September to go to the concert. I arrived after an overnight flight, I was sleepy but wired and spent the weekend laughing, dancing, and hanging out with a friend I had met in Los Angeles. We had a most enjoyable weekend together, she introduced me to some of her local recovery friends, and before I knew it the weekend was over and I was flying back to Los Angeles, I hadn't slept in 48 hours but I was filled with so much energy; happiness, and dread to be returning to my home.

October arrived and in it we celebrated Sarah Anna Anna's birthday by having a big party at a trampoline park, she had the best time jumping up and down, talking with her friends, she was so happy with the magical rainbow my little pony birthday cake her I had made her, she was so proud and happy, the only drawback was that her dad refused to attend her birthday party. I had invited his mom to come to her birthday party, i felt obligated, his mom just wanted to be close to her grandkids and her son spent his every moment hating his parents, so I invited his mom because Sarah Anna Anna wanted her grandma there, and it was her birthday. The night before the party Igor and I got into a bitter argument that left me in tears, and him promising not to attend his daughter's party. After the party was over the argument continued so leaving the kids with grandma I went to a meeting to clear my head, vent, and to find my fake smile to continue survival. The fights were getting worse, the in between somewhat happy moments were getting further away and harder to convince myself of their worth, I was unhappy and terrified.

Fall hit shortly after Sarah Anna Anna's birthday and it was my friend's sober birthday, the birthday was amazing, her and I had a great night acting silly and like kids, eating dessert, Sarah Anna Anna was with us and she basked in the attention and fun of hanging out with adults, she was always my plus one and she inspired me on how to have conversations. After the birthday celebration I started feeling weird. I was still exercising daily, I had gotten an early anniversary gift from Igor To a fancy gym for a month to try, while trying it, I signed up for personal training, I began pushing myself on the weights squatting heavier than I knew was possible, I was exerting myself physically more than I ever had before, I felt possessed by the desire to better myself, to be perfect, to look perfect, yet I wasn't, I spent hours at the gym everyday, I would bring the kids with me on weekends to avoid being at home, I was working towards a goal of being skinny yet I didn't know what skinny was. Towards the end of October I began to loose my steam for the gym, I took a spin class and afterwards it began to hurt to walk, I blamed it on not having cycle shorts, I blamed it on being fat, out of shape, but it got worse. I couldn't sit down, there was something wrong with my butt, but I couldn't let it hold me back. I was launching an exercise group to pair with my recovery group, and I couldn't let this stall my progress.

Abscess to Fistula

November arrived and with it my realization that there was something wrong with my left butt cheek, my perfect butt was disfigured, I panicked, was this fate, I would never be loved looking like this, and it hurt. It hurt so bad, but I was stubborn, I hated doctors, so I took a break from exercising for a few days certain it would fix the problem; two days later I started running a fever and I felt week, the lump had grown and was even more painful, I resigned myself to visiting a doctor. I made the appointment for a few days later, enough time to pass incase I was magically cured, at home I pretended nothing was wrong, the kids were curious why we had stopped going to the gym, but they were also happy to not have to go to kids zumba classes. The day of the doctors appointment arrived and I was convinced I had a tumor, or an ulcer, or some other horrible diagnosis that would impact me for the rest of my life, it was only fair after all that I had done to my body. I deserved as much. The doctors appointment led to no answers, she suspected it was maybe an abscess but it was under the skin and there was nothing she could do to help me, she suggested I just stay off it, not exercise and hope it came to the surface soon; this was just another reason why I disliked doctors. I said thanks and went home-I googled at home remedies to help an abscess ripen, I couldn't bear to continue this ongoing pain for weeks, it was impacting my life, I was a full time mom, my kids had expectations of me, I had expectations, sitting home was not how we did things. So I researched, I learned that if I rubbed essential oils on it it could help break open the skin to allow the abscess to ripen, it wasn't for the faint of heart, it meant I would be burning my skin, the only other alternative was an incision and drain but the doctor wouldn't do it-yet. So I began rubbing tea tree oil on it, I would take a bath after ten minutes of agony and within two days the abscess was at the surface, I was resigned to laying on my stomach, sitting was unbearable, the gym was long forgotten, driving was unbearable but necessary.

Veteran's Day weekend coincided with Igor's birthday and I spent it crying in pain, by the end of the weekend I was being driven to urgent care, at urgent care the doctor asked me why I had waited so long to have the abscess treated, I couldn't be bothered to answer. I was in pain, I was in agony, I was mortified at having a male doctor looking at my private areas, but i had no other choice, I needed this to heal, the doctor told me to brace myself that it was going to hurt. I nodded and then I was laying on my stomach, the doctor put a shot directly into the abscess to numb it, though as he explained it doesn't really help but maybe it would help me-it didn't, I let the tears fall silently, holding my breath as he cut into the skin on my butt, cut open the abscess, then applied pressure draining it. Once finished he suggested over the counter pain medicines and I was sent home. It was two weeks until Thanksgiving and I was hoping this would mean it would heal and I would be back to exercising soon. I made a follow up appointment to have the cotton gauze removed from the wound in a few days and was sent home to take baths every 4 hours. As soon as I reached home the gauze fell out, by the next day the wound was closing, I called the doctor who assured me it should be fine, so I kept following the rest of the directions, but I knew something was wrong. I could feel every movement, everything inside me was screaming it wasn't going correctly.

The next week dawned and with it excruciating pain was emitting from my wound, it wasn't healing, it was getting worse, I went back to the Urgent care who wouldn't touch it and told me to toughen it out, a few days later I went to my primary care doctor who referred me to a general surgeon, and by the end of the week I was frustrated. The doctors weren't listening to me, my wound was painful, my life was horrible, I couldn't drive, I couldn't walk, I wasn't interacting, I was depressed, anxious, and horribly tired of the emotions flowing from me. I finally got to see the general surgeon, Igor drove me, he was sick of me being incapable of doing stuff, he was making jokes that I was exaggerating the pain comparing it to him having a hemorrhoid a few months previously which he knew was way worse than what I had, and could even be compared to giving birth to babies. I ignored him, I knew if I responded I would cause more problems than it was worse, I let him pretend he had experienced worse than me and I sat in the surgeon's office hoping for good news. The surgeon diagnosed me fast, he informed me he was going to drain it again, he didn't believe in packing the wound, he would just cut it large enough that it wouldn't close for a few days. I said okay, he didn't put a shot in the abscess like the other doctor, he instead used 5 shots around the abscess area before using his scalpel to cut deep into the abscess and nearby area making a cross pattern on my skin, pushing it open and draining it. I again cried silently, and he finished quickly commenting that I was brave by not even making a sound, I smiled and said thanks, I would see him in a week. He mentioned to me that abscesses can lead to fistulas in about half the cases but he was positive it wouldn't happen to me, I again said thanks and left the office. It was a few days before Thanksgiving and I knew I wouldn't be making a big dinner this year, I was in pain, I could barely walk, and I was depressed.

Thanksgiving was a quiet day for our family, I managed to heat up a turkey that was pre cooked along with the basic sides, I made the best of it, the kids were happy, and that made me happy and bring me a bit out of my depression. After Thanksgiving I drug myself from bed enough to take the kids to the beach, to have some fun, I was in pain, and I knew my abscess was turning into a fistula, and I also knew it was out of my control so I focused on making the best of it. My butt constantly ached, but I started going back to AA meetings, I took pain pills like candy, and I continued on with my life. My sober birthday was approaching and I was excited though apprehensive, I had been working the steps of AA consistently and was at a standstill on steps 11 and 12, my sponsor and I were at a point where we were friends and sponsor/sponsee, I had my own sponsee, and she knew I was depressed. I had a trip planned to travel to Washington state with the kids and I was debating not going because of the abscess; but a few days before I assured the kids I would go so on my sober birthday the kids and I left for Washington, Igor was supposed to go but as usual he didn't want to, he didn't want to see his parents, and he wanted a break from his family.

The trip to Washington proved to be a good mental boost for the kids and I, we stayed with the in-laws, the first night I went to a meeting with a sober friend from an online group, she introduced me around, and I got told happy sober birthday, it was acknowledged by them and by my Cali sober family, even if Igor didn't, the kids, friends and my sober family did. The week in Washington was spent visiting museums, local tourist attractions with the kids, traveling to Seattle to hang out with sober friends, attending a comedy show, and traveling to the Sarah Anna Anna to play in it, I ignored my abscess, I ignored the fact that I was leaking liquid and felt disgusting, I ignored the pain, the discomfort, the smells and continued on for the sake of the kids and even for myself and my mental state. The day before we left the in-laws had a party where they drank and invited their friends over to show off their grandkids, it was boring, but I smiled and got through it, I couldn't wait to leave. The next day finally arrived and the kids and I drove to the airport stopping at my dad's grave to say our respects before boarding the plane and flying back to California.

Once back in California I went to the doctor who confirmed I had a fistula, a peri-anal fistula, he said he couldn't tell me more than that without surgery. I wanted surgery but our insurance was horrible so trying to be considerate based on how much money we had spent during the year- I waited till after the new year for surgery. Christmas and New Years took forever to pass, the highlight being watching the kid's faces on Christmas morning after Santa Claus had visited, bringing joy to their lives. Christmas and New Years were the highlights of the past few months and I basked in the simple joys of the holidays with the kids and puppies.

The New Year came and finally I could schedule surgery, the fistula hurt, I constantly had a fever, but I refused to let it completely control my life. I started exercising again spraying mass amounts of body spray on myself, taking showers 3 or 4 times a day, and 2 weeks into January I was going to have a fistulectomy. Igor took a few days off work to take me to surgery, and the morning dawned early, he was angry he had to wake early to take me to surgery, I didn't care. I went into surgery nervous and with an angry guy waiting for me in the waiting room-as usually he was resentful for being stuck with the kids as I was being put to sleep. Surgery went well with no complications, the surgeon was able to determine my fistula ran through my sphincter muscle and therefore based on his diagnosis he was unable to lay open the fistula like he had previously told me, as a matter of fact, he decided to insert a cutting seton inside that would slowly cut through the muscle which he declared would cause minimal cutting, minimal harm, and should fix the fistula without causing me incontinence. He told me all of this as I was awakening from anesthesia, he told me these things knowing I would have no memory of this and knowing I didn't have someone standing beside me to remind me. Eventually I was released, I was gently reminded to take baths every 3 hours, to rest, to stay off my feet, and to keep the wound clean; I was to follow up with the doctor in two weeks.

Abscess surgery to frustrated woman

The first few weeks passed quickly, I laid in bed on my stomach, I watched movies, I made podcasts, posted in my online groups, and texted friends while helping the kids with homework-Igor had thankfully offered to drive Sarah to school and Danny was sweetly walking to school daily. At the middle of the second week post surgery Igor told me he was going to his companies retreat for a week, he asked if I would be okay, I looked at him knowing there was only one suitable answer, so I said yes and away he went for the week leaving me home alone, in pain, healing, and caring for the kids. I couldn't drive because of the pain I had from having my butt cut open. Once Igor left for his retreat in Palm Springs the kids and I reached a mutual decision they would both stay home with me, I couldn't drive Sarah to school and being fair I decided to let Danny stay home as well, they were both excited to help me. I had a doctors appointment coming up and so I reached out to a friend to drive me to the doctor, I was growing frustrated at being helpless but I knew I had to ask for help, she agreed and took me to the doctor. After the doctor's appointment feeling the need to reconnect with women in the program of AA I arranged for ladies to come to my house to have a meeting, the kids were asked to go to their rooms with the puppies and the ladies arrived bearing snacks, laughter, and talking, it was a much needed reconnection to women sober like me, and women willing to listen to all that I've been through mainly curious as to why I was not having help from my spouse. I shrugged off their questions and focused on the message of the meeting, staying sober no matter what, using the steps, the tools of recovery to stay sober, and connecting with the ladies.

The rest of the week flew by and with it the kids proved to be the most amazing helpers, cleaning, bringing me drinks, offering to cook, and just keeping me company, but they hit a snag, Danny got sick, and after two days of coughing and fever I ubered him to the doctor, I didn't want a repeat of whooping cough. Ubering to the doctor was simple and the doctor prescribed some antibiotics and away we went back home to decide which take out restaurant we would eat from that night and which movie we would watch together. Eventually Igor came back home from his retreat filled with happiness and laughter, jokes about getting wasted with the boss's son, and jokes about being drunk in general, I was happy for him for enjoying his time, but I had needed him and he wasn't there to help me-again. Something had come over him at the retreat though, while he had been gone I had been researching alternative methods of treatment for fistulas, my healing had started producing ill effects, incontinence, more pain, and a lot of discomfort, I was getting desperate, I just wanted to be back to normal. I was tired of lying around, I was tired of feeling like garbage, so I made a pact with myself to get out of bed.

The next week I dove into researching more methods of treating a fistula, I hated not being able to control my bathroom urges, I hated smelling nasty even though I was assured no one could smell me, I hated the constant leaking and need to have fresh clothes with me at all times as if I was a toddler, life was unbearable, it felt like I was a drunk again, shame, remorse, guilt, self hatred, lack of self-confidence had returned with a vengeance. I started working out again to combat the feelings, I started driving myself places, I got the kids back on track in schools, and I started going back to my alcoholic meetings, but a spark inside me was dying. I felt hopeless and filled with despair, I obsessed about the possibility of traveling to India for treatment and mid February I broached the subject with Igor, I requested him to consider me going, I requested him to please let me go, it would mean sacrifices on his part, but I really needed the treatment, I was approaching 31 and looking at incontinence for the rest of my life, I couldn't bear that. He said he would think about it, in the meantime, I began searching for a new car, my current car's lease was coming to an end and my birthday was coming up so we were going to call it a birthday gift to me, I searched as obsessively as I did on alternative fistula treatments until I found the perfect car I wanted, a subaru outback, I was excited because I hadn't gotten to choose my own car in years.

Bachelorette party and tragedy

March came I was counting down the days until my next birthday though I figured as usual it would be a quiet affair but this year I refused to ask ever again for a birthday cake, I still regretted last years having to ask multiple times for a birthday cake, I was excited for the car, and I was happy to be back to working out even if I felt nasty about it. I was counting down the days to my friends bachelorette party which I had decided to attend even with the fistula, I needed the break, and I was hoping that Igor would agree for a trip to India.

March 7 my friends and I loaded up our cars and drove to the Long Beach airport, we were traveling to North lake Tahoe for a weekend of snowboarding, gambling, and fun, I didn't gamble but I was excited for a girl's trip. We boarded the plane wearing silly wigs and counted down until we landed in Tahoe. Igor was watching the puppies and kids, my puppy Chester had been sick so I was hoping he would keep a close eye on him. Once we landed at the airport I received a phone call from Igor, Chester had been rushed to the vet, he had woken up late and Sarah had told him the Chester wasn't moving, once Igor went downstairs Chester was weak, not breathing, he carried him to his car after trying to warm him up, Chester died on his way to the vet, though once at the vet they placed him on life support. I was hysterical, I had never cried so much in public before, I had never cried like that in front of people, yet I lost control, I was so sad, and I was the one who had to make a choice, did I want him to keep the puppy on life support or let him die. Standing in the airport hundreds of miles away, about to embark on a weekend that was supposed to be filled with happiness my dog died, I should have taken him to the vet before I left, I should have insisted and went against Igor's wishes and got him help, but I didn't, instead of trusting my instincts my favorite most loveable dog died and I wasn't there for him.

The weekend continued on, I was designated driver, I was the one who knew how to drive in snow and it was supposed to snow all weekend, but the car wasn't large enough, the original 15 seater was not all wheel drive and so we got to large SUVS, I would haul the 8 of us going snowboarding and another woman would drive the non boarders, after loading the cars we began the hour drive to the lake from Reno, we stopped along the way for lunch and afterwards made it to the cabin. Rooms were assigned and I was volunteered to share a bed with my friend, thankfully, and I finally took a moment to myself, I looked like crap, my fistula was bothering me, and I had to pull myself together. After a few minutes I went downstairs where we sat around to menu plan for the weekend, to get started on bachelorette games, the first being grocery games, we split into 4 teams each with a list of 12 items we had to find, and once at the grocery store we raced around, first one to finish got an extra oreo. My team and I mutually agreed to not run, to take our time, and to laugh at the others, it was fun watching them run around like crazy, we were the last team, but we also got everything off our list, we all went outside in the snow, loaded up the cars and drove back to the condo.

Four of us decided to go snowboarding the first night so while the others unpacked and assigned who was cooking and doing what we loaded our snowboards, got our gear, and left to go snowboarding. I hadn't been snowboarding in a while, I was nervous because of my fistula, I was nervous at how my knees would hold up. We drove out to Boreal Ski resort, the snow was beginning, the roads were icy, and I was happy to be distracted from the fact of my dog dying. We arrived, got our gear and walked to get our lift tickets, I got anxious, I was excited, and nervous, these women all were great at skiing and boarding, and I wasn't, but I didn't care, I was there to have fun. We boarding the ski lift and went up the first run, exiting the lift I managed to shove a woman out of the way as I slid off, we laughed and away we went, the first run is always nerve racking. My legs were shaking, my breath was fast, my heart was going to come out of my chest, I was going over in my head how to stop, how to turn, how to go, I took a breath, let it out, and started going down. I am terrified of heights, but I just went with it, and going with it was my mantra for the weekend; that first run was a preview of how my weekend would go.

I spent the weekend in the moment, focusing on snowboarding, driving, eating food, drinking cup after cup of coffee, and laughing. I was able to grieve in a healthy way for my puppy, and have fun, drinking alcohol never crossed my mind, staying connected and enjoying the girls trip was the focus. The weekend flew by and before we knew it we were boarding the airplane for the trip home, Igor texted me as I was boarding, he was angry-again. It was nothing new, but I was so tired and sad, he was mad that I trapped him in marriage, he was mad and accused me of getting pregnant on purpose, he was mad that his son was austistic, he blamed me for everything. It was nothing new but it was exhausting, I argued back, I informed him he killed my dog, I was angry, upset, I was crying and hiding behind my sunglasses. Luckily the plane took off and I couldn't talk to him for an hour, I was upset, I was tired of the same old argument, the same inability to get over things, I was tired of him guarding his phone like it was his most prized possession, of him informing me that I must constantly be grateful to him for babysitting kids, for being there. I was tired of so much, so tired that I slept the hour home, and at the airport I put on my fake smile, pretended things were okay, and dodged questions from my friends.

Driving home, I dropped off everyone who had carpooled with me at their respective houses, and continued on to my home. I was dreading facing Igor but looking forward to seeing the kids and other puppy, I got home, Igor was as usual on his computer completely ignoring me and the kids and doing what he does best-playing video games. I gave hugs, and gave souvenirs to the kids, we unpacked my bags and played a few games on the PS4, eventually after his game was over Igor ventured downstairs and sat on the couch, I asked the kids to go play with some toys so I could talk to their dad. Igor and I had a stare off, I finally broke the silence, I was tired of him bringing up the past, he didn't believe me back then, he didn't believe me now, I didn't get pregnant on purpose, I didn't trap him, he made his choices, he played a part in my pregnancy and he needed to suck it up and get over it or he needed to divorce me. I was tired of him bringing up the same argument over and over, I was tired of him using the same crap to bring misery in my life, in our lives, I was tired of him risking making our kids feel unwanted, I knew I was unwanted, but I couldn't bear for the kids to feel that way.

A few days passed by and things went back to the relative normal, Igor and I got along, and we pretended everything was okay. A few days after the few days Igor approached me, he told me I should decide on which doctor in India, I could go and get treatment done. I was excited and hopeful, I couldn't wait to go, he asked me which city I was going to go to and I told him I had decided on Bangalore, his coworker was from there and knew a friend who could assist me in checking out the doctor, hotels, and the location of where I should stay. I booked airline tickets right away before he could change his mind, I began looking for hotels to stay in and I reached out to the new acquaintance, he promised to check out my hotel, doctor, and get back to me. I was excited to be planning my trip, it was a week until my birthday ,and I was going to begin my travels the day after my birthday.

India

March 24, 2019 I woke up early to excited kids, it was a Sunday and they were excited to celebrate mom's birthday, where was the cake and presents, Snow loves cake and presents-whether they're hers or not. I smiled and said thanks for the birthday wishes, we snapped some photos together as a family, Danny, Snow, and I, and waited for their dad to wake up. I reminded them that I was going to be leaving for India the next day to seek treatment for my fistula, they knew how much I had been through, how much I've struggled, they're smart kids and especially Danny is in tune with my feelings. We planned out the day, we were going to go to the dog park and maybe by the time we got home dad would be awake, we loaded up, got the puppy in the car and away we went. Our first stop was starbucks for birthday drinks for everyone including a puppy frappuccino for Elsa; we arrived at the dog park and had an enjoyable few hours before venturing back home to be met with the repercussions of not cooking breakfast for Igor. It was what it was and I just let it pass, I was leaving the country the next day and I was refusing to fall into the anger trap, I took a breath and smiled and offered to cook immediately. I didn't mention or remind him it was my birthday, what would be the point. I made breakfast for him and myself, my favorite foods, grits, eggs, bacon, potatoes, tortillas, and sausage for the kids and we all sat around the table to watch TV and eat the food. The kids asked him what he got me for my birthday and he told them he bought me a car, he is paying for me to go to India, but to celebrate we could go out for teppanyaki which was perfect for all of us. The rest of the day passed by in a blur, Danny spent his day on the computer growing more quiet, Snow spent the day close to me playing her phone, and towards evening we all played a fighting game on the PS4 together before getting ready for dinner out.

Dinner out was a fun affair, the chef cooked beef, shrimp, chicken, rice, and vegetables in front of us, he made the volcano flame extra large to make the kids excited, and the kids and I laughed and smiled, it was a great birthday dinner, we left the restaurant filled with food and happiness. Igor had spent the time in the restaurant drinking so his mood was mellow and loose, and basically on good terms. He drove us home and once there the kids assisted me in ensuring my suitcase was all packed up for my trip, they gave me suggestions on souvenirs to bring them back, and I assured them that I would call them daily. I was going to miss them, I had never been away from my kids for so long and I was nervous about being gone for three months, but I was excited to get cured from the fistula. We went to bed early because I wanted to arrive at the airport three hours early, my flight was scheduled to leave at 5 pm we were going to leave our house at 1 pm to make the 60 mile drive to Los Angeles Airport getting me there around 2pm. Our drive to the airport was uneventful, Igor drove like a maniac speeding past other cars, driving at times double the speed limit, stressing me out about trusting him to get the kids back home safely, how was he going to care for the kids alone, but along the way he mentioned his mom would be arriving in two days to care for the kids and I was reassured they would be safe and fed and cared for because both Igor and I both knew he hated having to take care of the kids, as it was each mile closer to the airport, his attitude grew, he was getting resentful about being in charge of the kids, I was the one who was supposed to do everything and here I was going off on a vacation. I just sat there talking to the kids who were getting emotional, scared, and nervous, I talked to them about what they would do while I was gone, by the time I was back we would be packing things up to move to Florida and begin in a new place.

We arrived at the airport before 2 pm and the kids got out the car to hug me goodbye, I squeezed first Danny then Snow and finally Igor walked around to hug me, I told the kids I loved them, I said farewell, and grabbing my suitcase I walked into the international terminal in LA with a few tears falling silently down my cheeks and the knowledge that I was about to go through major changes in my life and I was going to do it alone. I checked into my flight and made my way to the security line, the major reason why I had arrived three hours was this, as usual for LAX the line was super long, I got in line, untied my shoes, took off my jacket and belt in preparation and continued waiting; 90 minutes later I was finally at the security point, and got through making my way to my gate to wait for my flight. I got my starbucks, browsed the duty free shop, walked up and down the airport multiple times, called a few friends saying bye to them, and walked to my gate, in time to be notified it was delayed by half an hour, sighing, I found a seat and began waiting.

I eventually boarded the plane, 16.5 hours from LAX to Dubai, I had booked a window seat and was excited to be able to get my seat, get comfortable, and awaiting take off. I sent texts to my kids, a text to Igor, popped in my earbuds, took some melatonin to promote sleep, and watched as we taxid to the runway and began our flight to Dubai. The flight to Dubai was uneventful, I slept for about 4 hours, enjoyed some food, watched most of the avenger movies, and slept some more, we landed in Dubai at 7 pm the next day, March 26, getting off the plane I was welcomed to the country by getting thoroughly searched before taking the bus to my next terminal to catch my connecting flight to Bangalore that would leave in 7 hours, too little time to leave the airport according to Dubai Customs, so I set about to walk the entire terminal to keep from falling asleep. I walked up and down the airport, I went into every store, checked out every trinket, shop, food place, I had 4 cups of coffee, snacks, and I still had 3 hours to burn! What was I supposed to do, at one point I found a chair and reclined in it watching comedies on my phone, sending messages to friends in the United States, I began counting down the minutes until I could walk to my gate to board the next flight. Eventually it was 130 AM and I could go to the gate and wait for the last 30 minutes before boarding my connecting flight, I was ecstatic I was almost to India and I was sober, surviving, and awake. I boarded the flight to Bangalore exhausted, the steward took mercy on me and moved passengers around so that the two seats next to me was empty for the 4 hour flight, I stretched out and slept and arrived in Bangalore only a little worse for wear, excited, and exhausted. I got through customs in India relatively easy, the customs agent spoke enough English to get that I was just visiting and exploring the city and I had nothing to claim, I walked out of the airport to the Uber booth and began my journey to my hotel. Riding in Uber my first thoughts of India, Bengaluru were that it was so loud, everyone used their horns, non stop, and when they weren't honking were driving in the middle of the road, on the side, never in lanes, they didn't seem to follow traffic rules, red lights could mean green, green could mean to stop, there were cows walking in the road, the traffic was horrendous, and I'd been in Los Angeles traffic plenty of times and comparatively

LA traffic was a joyride. It took about 2 hours to go the 47 kilometers from the airport to my hotel, I was nervous about what it would be like, I was told it was in a dusty part of town, but I figured this was India and I was told by people everything was dusty so I just assumed that was normal. I arrived at the hotel eventually after being asked for directions on how to get there, after the uber driver asked police and locals for help, I was exhausted and confused, but I dragged my suitcase inside, took a breath and prepared myself for the worse, from the outside, I was not hopeful for the accommodations and I was glad I had brought bleach wipes, gloves, and sanitizer with me. I got checked into my room with broken English, they demanded all of the payment for the first month up front so I handed over my card and was shown my room. There were bars on the window, there was dirt on the table, the bathroom was disgusting and missing a seat, the bed looked clean, but I was doubtful, I had no water, and I couldn't drink from the tap, it was 3pm and too early to go to bed. I booked an uber after depositing my suitcase, grabbed my laptop and left to go to a mall I had been recommended to visit. Food, water, a tea kettle, snacks, and extra cleaning supplies were a necessity, I arrived at Orion mall and was happy to see familiar sights and stores, I walked around the mall and found a restaurant to eat at. After eating I grabbed a starbucks to help me stay awake and researched where the local grocery store was- there was one in the mall so I did my first shopping in an Indian grocery store. You had to have you fruit weighed before checkout and people skipped you if you didn't stand close enough, they ignored me just as easily as they skipped me in lines, getting help was almost impossible at times, the fruit and vegetables had different names than I was accustomed to, Eggplants were called brinjals, bell peppers were called capsicum, and so much more, it was amazing and fun to explore the store. I eventually got what I wanted and checked out, I booked the uber back to the room, and after the driver got lost twice we finally arrived there, I hauled my bags up to my room and began cleaning the room so that I could sleep. It was 7 pm, I could barely keep my eyes open, 2 packs of bleach wipes later the table, toilet, and sink were clean and sanitary, the bed was sprayed multiple times with disenfanct, and I passed out on the bed in my clothes at 8 pm after calling home to let the family know I was safe, in my room, and exhausted.

Two am came and I received a phone call from the hotel's manager, he was speaking fast and in a heavy Indian accented

English about me needing to change rooms, pay more money, something something something, I hung up the phone confused, and unsure what I had heard other than that he was requesting more money, changing rooms, and to see him in the morning. I was livid, I was jet lagged, sleeping, and he woke me up in the middle of the night, I was awake so I began searching for alternative places to stay, I had heard of things like this happening, but I couldn't believe it was actually happening, because I was female, western? It didn't matter, I booked an airbnb for the night after next, and I booked a different hotel for the following night, I packed up my belongings, and fell asleep until 8 am, when I woke up. I ventured downstairs to find the manager and request a refund and to check out of the horrible place. I told the front desk I was checking out and they immediately requested me to stay, I had booked a month why was I leaving, I just shook my head and asked them for the remainder of my stay's money back so that I could leave immediately. I wasn't happy and I was not in the mood to deal with this. The manager ventured downstairs from his office and requested I speak with him privately, so I spoke with him, he asked me why I was leaving, he requested more money to stay in my current rom, I refused, I kept saying no, I asked over and over again for the money back, he kept ignoring me, he asked me where my husband was, if he could speak with my husband so that he could talk sense into me; I stood up and requested for the final time my money, I was here alone, it was my money, and I didn't need a man, a husband to talk sense into me. He brought in a woman to talk sense to me, I refused to listen, gathered my belongings, booked and uber, and he followed me downstairs, he eventually gave me money back and I left the place the woman following me to the uber begging me to stay. My first night in India was not pleasant, but it has taught me that I was not in the United States, and as a woman I wasn't going to be respected by many, especially since I was alone.

I moved to a new hotel for the night in a popular part of town, I dropped my bags and arranged to meet a woman from Australia who was here in Bangalore for fistula treatment as well, she was going to introduce me to some other fistula warriors and we would all have lunch together, I was nervous but happy to meet some fellow travelers from around the world, she was from Australia, I was from California, and they were from parts of Israel. We met at an Italian place and enjoyed lunch together, laughing, talking fistulas, and treatment, they gave me some helpful tips for my upcoming meeting with the doctor in the evening.

Butt scans and friends abroad

After lunch I began my trip to the doctors office, it would take about an hour or so to travel the 9 kilometers to the doctor's office in traffic, I was surprised, it wasn't far yet it was so far, yet another lesson in Bangalore traffic. I got in my car and drove to the office arriving a few minutes earlier, I met some other fistula warriors who would become constants in my life for the next few months, and I waited patiently to meet the doctor. The doctor arrived twenty minutes after the scheduled time and by that time I realized he told everyone to arrive at 6pm and would call people back accordingly, I was called back right after he arrived. The examination was an unpleasant as any other examination of a fistula has been, it meant letting go of more of my dignity, placing my feet up high in stirrups, and taking a breath while staring at the ceiling fan and getting poked. It wasn't pleasant but if it meant I was going to be cured I was willing to endure it, the meeting with other patients had prepared me for what was to come, they had also inspired in person faith as they were healing, and some almost finished healing from far more complicated fistulas than I had. After the examination the doctor and I went into his office to discuss treatment, it was the moment of truth, could he help me?

The doctor assured me he could help me, he gave me a prescription to have a total rectal ultrasound scan the next day, he gave me directions on how to pay for treatment and told me not to worry if it took a few days, things were a bit more complicated right now in regards to money due to elections happening in India and to take my time, he said to come back in the evening after the scan and we would schedule the date of the procedure. I went back to my hotel for the night, called my family, and told them the hopeful news; I went to bed early that night in order to wake up early for my scan the next day, and in order to be able to drop off my bag at the airbnb before going. It was going to be a busy day but I just knew I had to be at the scan center by 930 according to the doctor to ensure I wouldn't be there all day waiting, westerners tend to have to wait longer than others did.

Waking up early in the morning, I checked out of my room, grabbed my suitcase and began hopefully my last switch of hotel rooms for a while, I was moving 2 kilometers away from the doctors office which would mean less traffic, and would make post surgery an easier experience. I met the airbnb hosts who spoke perfect English and turns out used to live in the same city as I had in the Bay Area, Fremont, worked at a tech company I am very familiar with, and were super kind people. I dropped my bag and went to the scan center, I was the first to arrive and after broken English we established why I was there, I was told to wait, so I sat down with my book in hand, and began to read; it was 930 AM on a Friday morning. By 1030 I was getting bored but I was warned by the group that I would wait at least 3 or 4 hours and to be patient, if I asked I would likely be there even longer. So I waited, at 1230 I had just finished my book I had brought with me, and was making tentative plans to meet with the Fistula group at a members hotel room for a late lunch at 230pm, five minutes later I was called back for the scan. Getting the scan was an uncomfortable experience and if you ever find yourself needing a TRUS scan, relax, if you don't relax you'll regret it, and if you do relax it goes by much faster, the scan revealed my fistula, it also revealed the US surgeon had cut through my entire sphincter muscle which explained why I was having incontinence, and it showed the length of it, the size, and positioning, the doctor doing the scan didn't give away any information, instead he printed out my results, and sent me on my way. I took pictures and sent them as a text message to my doctor in preparation for the nights appointment and then I made my way to lunch with the fistula group.

Lunch was held at a hotel room one of the Israeli members stayed in , it was super nice and had its own kitchen, they had prepared lunch for all of us, a nice taste of Israel in Bangalore. We all had almost the same diet restrictions once we began treatment, no meat, some of us including myself could eat eggs, and some of us, like me, were not supposed to eat or drink dairy products. Lunch was hummus, egg shakshuka, and salad, it was amazing, and it was so much fun talking in English to everyone, I met another woman who was from Canada, and we passed around my scan results, one of the men got out his scan and we compared them for a while. We discussed the results in length, talking about treatment and they all commented on how mine seemed relatively uncomplicated compared to theirs, and I was amazed at what they had been through, it made me immensely grateful I hadn't continued trying western operations, one was more than enough, other than my sphincter muscle being cut, I hadn't had 10 surgeries, I hadn't had it for years and years, and it wasn't too close to my female parts. Around 4 pm I excused myself and headed back to the doctor sharing an uber with the women who were also heading to the clinic, they told me about how they had done their surgeries, advising me to bring pillows, books, snacks, and other various items with me if I elected to have it done under general anesthesia, or a spinal block; they also let me know that what needed to be sterilised was sterilised but the hospital was nothing like we were used to in Western societies, and in our opinions it could even be considered dirty, but to breathe, they had all had successes and I've had a tetanus shot so it'll be fine. I laughed, a part of me thought they were joking but then I remembered the clinic, so I thought on it the entire hour ride to the clinic.

At the clinic the doctor reviewed my scans, we talked about my sphincter muscle being cut and what that would mean for me, I was young so in theory it would heal to a certain extent but the muscle had been cut, Kshar Sutra treatment could help it, that's why I was here to use the ancient Indian Medicine and treatment. I said okay, I listened to him as he laid out his plans, he would do a partial lay open of the fistula tract and since it wasn't too deep it wouldn't be too complicated, I was looking at 3 months or so of treatment, a few kshar sutra thread changes, and of course the laying open of the tract. I had a decision to make, did I want to do the surgery in the clinic? Did I want to have treatment at the hospital? I needed to decide right then and there, the hospital meant staying the night by myself, I hated hospitals, and staying in a hospital in India terrified me. If I didn't stay in the hospital it meant having treatment in the clinic using just local anesthetic, shots into the butt. I took about five minutes, I was scared of the pain, but I was more terrified of staying alone in a hospital, so I told him I would have it done at the clinic, he said okay and sent me to the nurse to have blood drawn to figure out my blood type and we scheduled my surgery for April fools day, April 1, 5 days after arriving in India. I had a weekend in front of me to explore before I would have surgery on Monday. I reached out to Igor's coworker's friend in Bangalore and asked if he wanted to meetup and we agreed to meetup on Sunday evening for dinner before I had surgery on Monday, he asked me how I was doing and I explained all that had happened so far, he apologized for not being in town to help me,but he would make it up to me on Sunday and to call anytime, we hung up and I met up with the ladies from the group for dinner at the restaurant next to their hotel. We talked about things to do, and decided to hang out together on Saturday afternoon, we traveled to commercial street to do some shopping, and after commercial street one of the women and I, a woman I was fast calling a friend invited me to a local woman's house so that we could go to a wedding of her friends. I was excited, what an amazing way to spend a Saturday night, and the best part of all of this was, none of these people drank alcohol, it was like whatever essence of the universe had sent me to this place and entrusted me in a group of people who weren't drinking alcohol or using drugs.

My first Indian wedding, south Indian wedding was amazing, I was dressed in a local woman's clothes, a long skirt and a blouse showing off my stomach, it was baffling, it was frowned to show your cleavage but no matter your size, it was acceptable to show off your stomach, but I went with it and 7 of us piled into her tiny car to drive to the wedding. We arrived and were marched to the front to greet the bride and groom and congratulate them, posing for a photo, after which we were led downstairs and given food on a leaf, it was all vegetarian, and all the things that my friend and I had no clue what it was, and we were expected to eat with our hands. We sat there laughing at each other until the local friend took pity and asked in the local language for spoons for us to use, we were grateful, but more grateful we had already eaten and wouldn't have to each much of the food. After the wedding we took photos, looked around and went back to change into our own clothes and then headed back to our rooms. I was nervous about driving after 9pm alone in an uber but they assured me it would be fine. So I booked an uber and begged my friend to drop me off at my airbnb before she went on alone, I was still new and very nervous; she agreed.

Sunday dawned bright and early, it was my last day before surgery so I wanted it to be filled with things, I was assuming I wouldn't be walking for a while so I had gotten snacks, tea, and fruit to eat in my room, I had talked to my hosts and they were kindly offered to bring me to the doctor's office in the mornings to help me assuming I left at the same time as my host did to go to his office, I was grateful. I elected to go to a pyramid in an outstation I had read about online, it was supposed to be amazing and it was a great place to do meditation, I booked an uber and we started the 2.5 hour drive out there, along the way he got pulled over by the traffic police where the made him open his trunk and asked him a variety of questions, I sat there mutely afraid of what was happening and keeping my eyes on my phone. Eventually we started driving again and we went through small villages, passed lots of garbage and cows along the road, and we arrived, it was in the middle of nowhere with no cell phone service, I realized if the uber left I was going to be in trouble so I convinced the driver to wait 30 minutes while I went and looked around, I didn't feel up to meditating after all, I had just spent 2.5 hours in my thoughts, I was reflecting on the mornings conversation with Igor where he told me his coworkers husband was calling and harassing him and he was laughing about it, I was reflecting on tomorrow's surgery, and I was missing my kids. I got out of the car and walked the mile to the pyramid, I saw it, took a picture, and I returned to the car for the drive back to Bangalore, it wasn't the best adventure, but I saw a different side of Bangalore so I was happy. I returned in the afternoon to Bangalore, confirmed my plans with the guy Bobo, and rested until he would pick me up at 7pm.

At 7pm Bobo arrived to pick me up, he asked me what I wanted to eat and I asked him to take me wherever he wanted but I was vegetarian and needed to stick to that please. He agreed and he found us a nice vegetarian place to eat at, conversation at first was stilted, we sat across from each other both strangers, both quiet and smiling, eventually I asked him about his work, whether he had a family, how he knew Igor's coworker, and he proceeded to order some dishes for me to try in hopes I would have a few options of food I would enjoy during my stay. We had some potatoes, chapati, cauliflower, and some other food that to this day I can't recall what it was aside from spicy. After dinner we went for a walk nearby and looked at a famous street for shopping for western style clothing and items, we continued talking both becoming more animated in our conversation, I was happy to speak to a local who knew the customs and the language, as well as someone who knew my language perfectly. I asked him about getting a local phone number, and he offered to help me out as I hadn't been successful locally and I had forgotten to get a phone call from the airport when I arrived. After our walk we returned to the car where he proceeded to drop me off back at my airbnb safely and in a gentleman behavioral way. He said he would stay in touch and we would hang out again soon, I thanked him and left to go to bed, 7 am would arrive soon and I had surgery.

Kshar Sutra Ayurvedic Treatment

April 1 dawned bright and early, I was going to go to surgery, my new friend had kindly offered to ride with me to the clinic and sit with me, I was grateful, my morning had started off on a bad note, Igor had called me complaining. My closet wasn't perfectly organized, why couldn't I stack my clothes neat and orderly, why was I such a slob, he had hired a house cleaner to clean the house because my lazy ass couldn't keep a house clean before his mom arrived, he was paying for my trip how couldn't' I have been bothered to straighten things up. I was hysterical, he knew I was going to have surgery, he knew I was alone in a country and he just kept pushing my buttons, I wanted a drink, I wanted a friend, I wanted comfort, instead I got yelled and screamed at, I got put down, I was never good enough for this man, even 10,000 miles away, he had the power to make me feel like garbage, he had OCD, I didn't, he's known that for years yet he never forgets to yell at me. I pulled myself together as best as I could, I talked to the kids, and I booked an uber to come get me, along the way to the clinic, I picked up my friend and she right away knew something was wrong. I tried to hide it, I didn't want to dump my problems, issues on someone else but she gently poked me till I told her what had happened, she whipped out some essential oil and placed some on my wrist and told me to relax.

At the clinic the nurse checked me for allergies and after ten minutes I was sporting a new bruise on my arm from the check, thankfully I wasn't allergic and I was told to wait for the doctor to arrive. I waited with my friend in a room that was relatively clean, at 9 am the doctor arrived and I walked back to the room for surgery, I was nauseous, scared, and upset, my face was red from crying and I figured things couldn't get worse than they already were so I laid on the bed with my feet in the air and surgery began. 6 shots, some slicing, and the finishing touch of burning my skin and surgery was over 20 minutes after it had begun, I was walked back out to my room to lay flat on the bed for 2 hours to rest before I was allowed to leave. I was numb, I was still nauseous, but I had survived the pain. I experienced my first cauterizing experience, and I had a thread inside my fistula tract and the tract had been cut open, the journey of treatment had begun.

I went home 4 hours after I had arrived at the clinic, I was numb, I wasn't in pain, but I knew eventually the numbness would wear off and I would start feeling something. I was told that I was to do sitz baths 2-3 times a day, and to keep the area clean, I had to come in for bandage changes every day, and I needed to walk daily, but not the first day. I nodded and went home to rest, I ordered food once I arrived back at my airbnb, and my friend told me she would check on me later. I rested that day and night until about 2 am, something about 2 am seems to be and always has been the time of night where my life has major changes, whether it was sobering up from alcohol, coming from a blackout, or like this night when I receive a facebook message from Igor's coworker's husband, he wanted my phone number and email address to talk to me and send me something important relating to Igor. I sent him both and waited, I knew something was wrong, this was the man that had supposedly been harrassing Igor, why would he be speaking to me about his wife and Igor,his wife whom I considered an annoyingly stinky lady, who had always bugged me with her closeness and desire to talk to my kids and me. So I waited, I messaged my sponsor telling her I had a bad feeling, I was in pain from surgery and I was scared.

Within minutes I received a phone call from a man who was Igor's coworkers husband, he was angry, he was upset, he was ranting about Igor, ranting about an affair that had been going on for months with his wife, but he needed proof, he needed to know if the person on the tape was Igor, I agreed to listen to the tape and he disconnected the call. A few minutes later I received an email with an audio recording, the recording was about an hour long, I was sitting in the dark, my email open, my finger was hovering over the play button, I was conflicted over what to do, but in my heart I knew what I was going to do, I knew what I was about to hear, I was already in pain post surgery, I had spent the morning getting put down for not being good enough, and now I was going to hear the truth about something I had suspected for a few months-since playfully touching Igor's phone and his overreacting. I clicked play on the file, and right away I heard voices, I could tell the recording was hidden, they didn't know they were being recorded, the voice on the tape was Igor's and the other was his mistress, they were laughing and giggling. I continued listening, I listened to Igor talk about how much he loved another woman, how crap I was as a wife, how I was never intimate with him, how much he found the other woman was attractive, how he enjoyed every minute with her. I listened more and heard him talk about me, about hooking me up with her friend, about how her friend is handsome and what if he and I had an affair, I listened to word after word until the words stopped coming out and all that was left was the sound of their kissing and being intimate. I listened until I couldn't bear to listen anymore, it was painful, I felt like my heart was breaking, on the one hand I had talked about leaving him for years, I had talked to a divorce lawyer a year or so earlier, I had talked to my friend only weeks earlier about my frustration and desire to get out of the relationship, but I wanted it to be on my terms, not on his.

The Betrayal to Happy ever after

I called Igor after listening to the tape, he didn't answer, I left a message and I sent a text message, I called back the other man and confirmed what I knew, we talked briefly he was asking me my plans, what was I going to do. I told him I had no answers, but the one thing I knew was that Igor had done this once, probably many times, and he would do so again so would his wife. I wished him good luck, he promised to send me receipts from hotels they had stayed at, I said goodbye and hung up the phone. I was devastated, I was exhausted, and I was waiting for Igor to return my phone call. A little bit later Igor returned my phone call, he was sheepish and I asked him straight out if he cheated on me, he knew something was up, I asked him to honestly answer, he had promised me once upon a time he wouldn't lie about this so I was asking him now. He told me he had cheated with the woman, I asked him how long he had been cheating on me, how many women, how many times, how long has this been going on, how could he bring our kids around her, how could he live with himself? He told me he had been cheating for five years, he blamed me, my drinking, he then reminded me that men are inclined to cheat, monogamy isn't in human nature and what did I expect, he was loyal for 5 years and these things were flings, they weren't permanent, I was his love his life, couldn't I keep an open mind, what about an open relationship, he would live in California, I would live in Florida with the kids and once a month he would come to visit. I listened to him saying nothing, either he was pure cruel, or he was oblivious, what did he think I would feel or say, why would he act like it's no big deal? I hung up on him.

I stayed up all night, I texted the new guy acquaintance though it was super late asking if he would be willing to take me for a drive the next night-driving, riding, was a coping measure that helped me. I messaged my kids, I messaged friends, I posted in my online groups, and eventually it was morning and time to go to my first post surgery appointment. I messaged my new friend from the local group and together we went to the doctors office, again she noticed something was up but I wasn't ready to talk on the way to the clinic. We arrived at the clinic and I saw the nurse, I had my packing changed grimacing in pain, and waited while she saw the nurse. Afterwards she introduced another fistula warrior friend and we all decided to go explore a bit afterwards, he was a local, were wondering why I didn't want to rest but for me it was simple the less time I had to rest and think about everything the better. I eventually told her what happened, I told her about being cheated on, about it being my fault, about Igor's suggestion of an open relationship, she was kind, she listened, and she agreed we should go hang out and get my mind off of things. We spent the day hanging out, we went out to lunch, and had an amazing day in Bangalore, I told the new friend what had happened and he just listened, I had made two new friends.

At the end of the day when it was morning in the US Igor called me, but I couldn't bring myself to talk to him, I ignored his calls, I was thinking. I was confused at what I wanted in my life, I was a mom, I didn't want to be the one to tear the family apart yet I was internally being torn apart, cheating was the worst thing, the fact he had cheated with the same woman over and over again, the fact he had brought her around our kids was devastating.

My ego was bruised, I hated myself, I wanted to drink, I wanted to numb the pain, I wanted an outlet. I decided to try flirting, to try dating other guys, why not, he didn't care about me, he didn't want me, he told me hurtful thing after hurtful thing, I wasn't sexy enough, skinny enough, good enough in bed, I wasn't what he wanted as usual, he sent me messages, he called me, I was done. I didn't drink that day or night, instead I joined a dating app. I sought to numb myself but I didn't want to die. I wanted to numb myself but I didn't want to kill myself, what I didn't know at the time was even though dating wasn't poisonous it was killing a piece of my soul. I was falling to pieces and I didn't know how to glue myself together at the time.

The evening came around and the new friend was coming to pick me up, I was nervous, I was excited, I felt numb, I knew he was interested in me and I could play it, but if I went through with this I wasn't sure how I would feel on the inside, but I was going to go through with it anyways. He picked me up and told me we were just going to drive for a while, it took a while to get out of the city, we wound our way out eventually to a highway towards Hyderabad and he drove for a while, he talked to me, he asked me what was going on and I told him his friend was sleeping with Igor, he just shook his head and made a comment on if it doesn't impact the family then what's the harm. Except it did impact my family, I'm a piece of my family, I was more upset, I was vulnerable, I knew I was making a mistake yet I felt out of control, and so when he leaned over to kiss me I didn't stop him. We drove on in silence and eventually he kissed me again, he was attractive, he was bossy, and it was nice to have attention from someone who clearly found me attractive. We drove for hours that night kissing occasionally, he kept trying to take it further but I was hesitant, my mind and heart and soul were torn apart and I was confused. He brought me back to my airbnb and though I knew he wanted to come inside I used the truthful excuse that guests were not allowed and I went to bed alone.

The next day I read through my dating apps messages, I had so many it was shocking, maybe I was pretty, attractive, or it could just be I was a westerner in India, but I really didn't care; I made plans to meet up with a guy that evening, he seemed nice. I spent the day with my friends from the group, especially my woman friend was worried about me, but she also knew what I was going through so she was kind, supportive, and caring in a time of need. We talked about what I had done the night before, I showed her the guys picture and we giggled about his looks, she reminded me to be careful and to buy some condoms-just in case. After talking with her I walked from the clinic to the pharmacy to buy condoms, I think I shocked the pharmacist at buying condoms before noon, and also I was a white woman buying them. It made me laugh so I decided to be adventurous and catch the metro alone towards the park, the only problem ended up being when it came to cross the road to the metro station I got terrified, there were so many cars, so many cars honking their horns, it was nerve racking, I couldn't do it. I called my friend and she invited me to lunch and so instead of crossing the street I chickened out and booked an uber, I would practice the metro with her more before attempting it by myself.

I met up with a group of friends for lunch, we spent over two hours laughing, talking, and discussing treatment, asking me how I was doing, it was an enjoyable time together, after lunch, my friend and I caught an uber back towards her hotel together, I was tired of my airbnb so I wanted to see her room, I wanted to be closer to her and the other woman from Canada and I wanted to be next to a restaurant, my airbnb was great but the hosts texted me often asking me where I was, what I was doing, checking up on me, and at the moment that is not what I wanted so I was looking to move as soon as possible. I toured her room, I was happy with it and I booked myself into the same hotel, I went back to my airbnb retrieved my belongings, gave the host my keys, and departed. Once at the hotel I was put in the room next to my friend, I unpacked and got dressed for my first date in over 10 years, I was nervous and excited, I was apprehensive, my US life was a mess, my life was uncertain, but for now I was just going to enjoy myself. On the recommendation of my friends I asked the doctors permission to have sex, one of the most ackward messages I've ever sent, but I got the approval, I had the condoms, and I was ready to go out.

I wouldn't give the guy the address where I was staying so I walked half a kilometer down the road to meet him, it started raining along the way and I was happy to be wearing pants and a shirt, he was waiting for me, and thankful part two was he was exactly as his picture suggested. We said hello to each other, I was nervous to pronounce his name but I managed, we caught an uber and were on our way out for a night of watching a movie and drinking mocktails. The night passed by fast, he was a sweet guy who didn't push for more than a kiss, and the night was a success. I went back to my hotel and reached out to Igor, it was time to talk.

Talking to Igor went as I had expected he mentioned an open relationship again and I told him sure, lets try it. I asked him more questions about his affairs, and he asked me for the truth if I got pregnant on purpose, I just laughed, he had never believed me, what was going to change now? I hadn't got pregnant on purpose, he is not who I would have chosen to spend my life with, I had a whole list of things I wanted in a life partner and he didn't meet half of them, but I accepted him as he is cause that's what you're supposed to do in a relationship. I asked him why he cheated on me, I don't know why I was punishing myself but I needed to know why, why wasn't I enough, good enough, pretty enough, why wasn't I enough? He told me I wasn't good enough in bed, I wasn't attractive enough, sure I was pretty, but I was boring. He told me hurtful word, hurtful phrase after phrase and word. I was devastated but I wasn't going to show it. I couldn't, he had gotten enough tears from me. I wanted revenge. I wanted to make him feel the way I felt. I ended the conversation soon afterwards, I couldn't bear to continue talking with him.

Dating mishaps

The week passed by in a blur, I went on date after date, at some point I eventually slept with the guy I first met, it was okay, it was fine, yet I felt horrible inside. Why if I was seeking revenge was it hurting me, I felt like a slut, I felt like a nasty person, and I hated myself, I was seeking comfort, I was seeking words, encouragement, outside influenced to fill me up, to make me feel better about myself, but it wasn't working. I had stopped talking to my sponsor, I had stopped talking to my kids, I had stopped talking to anyone close to me, I hated being sober, I hated feeling all the emotions, the inadequacies, I wanted to be numb. I wanted to drink. I wanted drugs, though I hadn't really ever been into drugs, I needed, wanted to not feel anything, just for a while. I kept pushing through, I met with guys in the afternoon to walk the park, I would go hang out with my group of friends and tell them about my adventures, especially my new closest friend, she kept reminding me to call her anytime, and to keep her posted to stay safe. I was grateful. I was sober. I was hanging on by the barest of threads. I was drinking energy drinks like water to stay awake, I was still going for treatment but I lost all interest in everything except this form of punishment I was pushing on myself. I hated myself for meeting these guys, I was tired of it, I didn't want an open relationship, but I was so afraid.

A new week was beginning, I was going to go on one more date, I had already planned it and it was just to go to the movies so I figured why not go through with it. We met at the movie theatre, I had chosen to see Pet Sematary, the least romantic movie I could find in English. The movie went well, the guy tried touching me a few times, he tried kissing me, I succumbed to a kiss but I refused to let him touch me, he was a nice guy, but a bit on the dumb side. After the movie finished I thanked him, he asked me if I wanted to go dancing on Saturday night, dancing sounded great so I readily agreed, it was at a club so I wouldn't be alone with him, and I assumed it was no strings attached, I was a bit naive but I wanted to go. The rest of the week passed by, I relaxed, I started realizing I wasn't eating, the comments from the fiends commenting on how much weight I've dropped in a week we're sinking in, I couldn't remember the last time I had had proper food, I wasn't hungry, I was enjoying another form of punishing myself, but I agreed to eat a meal with a friend who paid close attention to how much food I was eating. Treatment along with depression, anxiety, self hate had made my appetite disappear.

Saturday was here, the day was spent with the group we wandered around Bangalore, we saw the Sultan's summer palace which was a waste of time and money, we ventured towards the flower market only to change our mind halfway there, and eventually we caught the metro, the metro was getting easier to ride, I had only almost died once by my arm almost getting caught in the door, and so I was feeling braver while riding it, also when it was just us ladies we could ride in the women's compartment which generally meant less crowding so it was becoming my favorite method of travel, also the lack of traffic was extremely appealing. After hanging out during the day we finished the day off with some vegetarian sushi and mocktails, Bangalore has some of the greatest mocktails I've ever experienced, I felt grounded and I was getting back to my sanity, and finding the answers I was seeking to the question if I wanted, if I was willing and if I could be okay with an open relationship, if I could continue accepting Igor and the relationship we were in.

Saturday night I prepared to go to the club, I was looking forward to dancing, I had the doctors permission to dance, to do yoga, to move, so I was excited. Dancing was one of my favorite things to do in the world and I couldn't wait to check out an Indian dance club. I arrived at the time given to me and I waited, I was supposed to be there at 9pm, yet the date was nowhere to be seen, I took a breath and stood awkwardly inside waiting for him. 5 minutes passed, 10 minutes, a guy approached me and asked me to walk inside with him, I declined, I was waiting for someone, 15 minutes passed and another guy approached me and struck up conversation I smiled, nodded, and listened all while growing impatient, was I being stood up? The insecurities came flooding back but still I waited, the date finally arrived at

925pm, and I was relieved, he apologized, he had gotten lost as he was driving a borrowed scooter that way he could drive me home afterwards. I smiled, took a breath, there was no way I was going home with him, he kept me waiting 25 minutes, and he was boring, maybe his dancing was better than his conversation but his tardiness was inexcusable. We made our way to the club and went inside, the party was just beginning, they had hollywood style music on, and I was so happy to hear songs I knew. We found a spot to stand, he wasn't ready to dance yet and I suspected he wanted to drink, but he said he didn't so I let it go. After 10 minutes of standing in the spot I was bored, I asked him to dance with me and he reluctantly followed me to the dance floor, I was sober, happy, and began dancing instinctively.

The club was a new experience, I began dancing with my date who was not the greatest dancer, who was wearing a baseball hat, and I was tired of dancing with him. I excused myself to go to the bathroom but he followed me, he was growing increasingly clingy and I was growing tired of it, but I had came with him so I smiled and went into the bathroom alone. A few minutes later I came out to my waiting escort and we went back to the dance floor, the music was great and I lost myself in the movement of it. I was dancing and smiling and while turning I noticed a guy standing a little bit away from me, he was standing next to a tall guy who was clearly checking me out, I smiled and continued dancing. The songs were playing, my date had noticed the tall guy checking me out and made a comment I laughed and said so what, lets just dance, ignore him. I changed my dancing I was thinking about the guy I saw, I wanted to see if he noticed me, I knew his friend had but I wanted him to notice me like I wanted air to breathe. I turned my back on my date and danced while seeking the guy's eyes, he finally looked at me and I smiled at him, he smiled back! I was so happy, he had the best smile I've ever seen in my life, it lifted my heart, my spirits, and I wanted to talk to him. I kept dancing with my date, the date though was tired of dancing he wanted a break, I didn't, I couldn't leave the dance floor yet. I moved us back so that I was closer to the guy, when I danced I could feel the guy next to me dancing, it was exhilarating, I was so happy, we said something to each other but it was loud and I couldn't hear. I wanted to talk to him desperately, I knew I needed to get rid of the guy I was with, so I again excused myself to the washroom, smiling at the guy I was interested in as I was leaving.

The washroom was packed with women, I had left my escort outside waiting for me, I was desperate to be rid of him, sad, and annoyed, a woman took mercy on me and asked me to smoke a cigarette with her, I didn't smoke but I knew it was an opportunity to get rid of the guy, so as we were exiting the bathroom I told him I was going to hang out with her and I would chat with him later, he said okay but he was going to wait for me, he wanted to escort me home, I shook my head and followed her to the smoking room. We stood inside for a while, she smoked a cigarette as I half heartedly pretended to smoke, sucking in air blowing out air. I eventually excused myself from her, thanking her for the conversation, cigarette, and short dance, and I went in search of the guy with the eyes. I walked to where he had been standing and as I approached I saw his tall friend notice me, I smiled at him and he smiled back, but I kept walking, his friend was beside him and I walked straight up to him and said hi. He was happy to see me, shocked I had approached him, I was shocked at myself, but I didn't care, his eyes, his smile, he was hot, he had a great voice, and his name was Neel. We connected instantly and began dancing, After dancing for a while I told him I was thirsty and he walked with me to the bar, I asked for water and he was shocked I didn't drink alcohol, and bonus neither did he; after getting water he invited me to his place and I laughed, there was no way I was going to his place, the past few weeks had been exhausting and I couldn't be that way anymore. We danced more and he asked me again, I wanted to talk to him, I wanted to get to know him, but I didn't want anything other than that tonight and I told him as much, he was cool with it, and I finally agreed to take the risk and go to his place.

We booked an uber and went to his place, we spent what felt like hours talking and laughing, hugging, and kissing, getting to know each other, I was hesitant on what to tell him but eventually I told him everything. He was younger than me, he was shocked to learn about kids and Igor, but he swallowed it, it was a lot to take in but he didn't ask me to leave. I was so scared I wanted to know everything about him, I felt so connected to him, but I was scared. I was in a bad situation, he had all the power and I was afraid to lose him, or worse afraid he would be like Igor. I took a breath and refocused on the moment, eventually he invited me to stay at a different place of his, and he drove us on his scooter to his home where he fed me with his hands and we fell asleep together on his bed with plans to go to the zoo the next day. I was happy to hear he wanted me to stay the night and also wanted to spend the day with me despite everything.

The next day we hopped on his scooter, stopping briefly for me to buy some pants and drove out to the zoo. We spent an amazing day together talking, laughing, and getting to know each other, everything we talked about clicked. If I were to list out my ideal soulmate he would have ticked off every box of it right then and there, but I was still sitting in that fear, I had just gotten hurt, and I couldn't bear to be hurt again. After the zoo we made plans to meet up later in the week and he dropped me off at my hotel. I was so happy to have met him, he was perfect and I wanted to spend more time with him. I had some mess to clean up, after he left I reached out to a few guys I had been talking to and cut off ties, the first guy I had met was moving to London and that made things easy. A few guys continued messaging me that week flirting with me but I wasn't interested, I had lost almost all interest, but I continued talking because I was sitting in that ever present fear. I had a few conversations with Igor and I was navigating the waters about telling him I wasn't okay with an open relationship, and in between exhausting conversations with Igor, and mild flirtations, I was texting the acquaintance Bobo, he was sweet, and his words were catching, he was also an insider to Igor's mistress so I wanted to know more. It was dangerous to talk to him, he was so much like Igor it was insane; but I kept up the conversation digging myself into a horrible situation with him that was complicated.

Falling in unexpected love

The week passed and by Thursday I was desperate to see Neel, Thursday night I fell asleep early after having not slept properly in weeks, and woke up to several missed calls from Neel-he wanted to see me, to spend time with me, so I arranged to stay in a room closer to clubs so that it would be easier for us to hang out. We met up and he brought me a belated birthday cake, it was the sweetest thing ever, we ate cake, and watched Game of Thrones together, and planned to go dancing the following night together, we spent every moment of the weekend together, and I knew then I was falling in love. Maybe it was too soon, maybe it was stupid, but I knew it was love, and I knew I couldn't, i had just been destroyed, I couldn't trust someone with my heart, my soul; yet here it was happening. I started texting Bobo that Monday more often, I was flirting, and I was trying to protect myself, I couldn't fall into love, it wasn't safe. Men were liars and cheats. A few days later I was spending with Neel and he found the messages, he was devastated, I was devastated, I cared for this guy yet I was hurting him, I hated myself, I was like Igor, I couldn't be this way. He forgave me, I'm not sure why, and I asked for his help to find me a permanent place to stay for the next few months and he agreed to help me; meanwhile I continued conversations with Bobo, I knew it was stupid yet I couldn't stop, I wanted to flirt, I wanted to feel wanted, and I wanted to hurt him, in my head it was a way to hurt Igor, completely unrelated but related. The beginning of May came, my closest group friend was declared fistula free, I was moving into an apartment and treatment for me was going well, I had a few thread changes, the pain wasn't as severe, I had a solid group of friends, and I was settling into my relationship with Neel. I broke the news to Igor that I wanted a divorce and he was angry, upset, and threatening towards me. I spoke with my mom and told her all about what had been going on, she made suggestions, mainly about money and protecting myself, I just wanted out, I wanted my kids, and I wanted to be divorced; she sent me some money to retain a lawyer and to help me survive as Igor began threatening to cut off all money to me. I was panicked but I wasn't going to do what Igor wanted me to do, even if it meant becoming homeless in a foreign country, I couldn't go back to him. The kids were safe, they were being cared for by their grandmother and were preparing to go to Washington state for the summer, I had been talking to them daily, missing them, and hearing about school and their excitement for summer.

Divorce, lies, betrayals, and abandonment

Divorce, lies, betrayals, abandonment leads to Happily ever after

I filed for divorce mid May, it occured after another confrontation with Neel, he asked me why I was flirting with Bobo, what my plans were, he was in love with me and he wanted answers, he deserved to know my intentions, I was watching myself from afar and I could see I was becoming like Igor and if there was one thing in the world, I didn't want to be it was to not be narcissistic, not be cruel, not be a cheater, not be cruel, I was scared, I was terrified of being betrayed, hurt, cheated on, but I gave up, I cut off the final ties and I focused on my future. Filing for divorce was terrifying, Igor didn't believe that I would do such a thing, what about the kids, the kids were his power play, how could I tear apart the family. I was an evil person, I was banging a guy in India, I had left behind my kids, and I was the one filing for divorce. Igor forgot about his part, he forgot about the pain, torture, the hurt, the tearing apart he did to me, and I was the evil dooer.

May was spent with so many ups and downs, one week was spent worrying about money to pay rent, to pay for groceries, the next was spent being sick, I was constantly stressed. I caught the stomach flu multiple times, my treatment was stalling, the pain was intensifying, I was miserable but in love, I was happy but terrified. The divorce attorney stopped taking my phone calls and ignored me for weeks as she typed of the documents, my sponsor told me I was making the worst decision of my life, my recovery friends in California all for the most part stopped talking to me except my best fiend, and my mom was furious with me. I couldn't go home, Igor was a constant domineering force, threatening, begging, manipulating me with words and actions. He was angry when I wasn't constantly thanking him, and furious that I was divorcing him, his friends had all assured him I would come begging him back, why wasn't I? He became convinced it was because I was in India, so if he stopped the money I would come running back to the US and he would be in control of me again. I couldn't do it. I wasn't finished with treatment, I couldn't let it all be in vain, I was having problems with my uterus, and I was sick, again.

My recovery was suffering, my sponsor kept sending me suggestions, beg me to go to the horrible meetings in India, telling me I was insane, telling me to stay with Ivan, to come home immediately. I couldn't do it, I wouldn't listen to her, she expected me to follow her directions blindly, Igor expected me to follow his directions blindly, my mom expected the same, my life, my world was filled with people dominating over me, what about my wants, my dreams, my desires? What about Britney?

By the end of May I was fed up, the divorce attorney had finally submitted the divorce documents to the court in California, and I was done with being in AA, done with my sponsor, done with fake friends, and domineering people in my life, I was done following peoples directives. I fired my sponsor, I cut myself off from AA, I established boundaries with my mom, and began ignoring Igor except in regards to divorce.

June began and Igor found his own lawyer, he suggested we work together on a settlement, divorce in California is a 6 month affair and it would be best if we could be amicable, I agreed. We began drafting up papers, he wanted me to move to Florida and I was hesitant to agree, things had changed, i didn't want to do whatever he wanted me to do anymore. We eventually created a settlement agreement, it was brutal, it wasn't fair, but I didn't care, I wanted out, I wanted a divorce, no matter what it meant giving up. It meant doing whatever Igor wanted, alimony, a house to live in, child support, splitting his retirement plan, it was great, the only exception was if I didn't come back when he dictates. Part of the settlement stipulated I had to be back in the US by the end of September, my problem with this was the simple fact that I was afraid to come back, I love my kids, I love living in the US, and having money is helpful especially as I hadn't established my recovery coaching business properly yet, my group while going great wasn't a huge source of income, and blogging was mainly for fun, so money was important for survival, but I couldn't agree with this, yet I had no choice. I signed the settlement and he signed acknowledgement of the divorce papers being served on him. I was relieved, six months from now I would be officially divorced.

THings in India continued on through June, Neel and I fell deeper in love, the early issues of our relationship, my cheating, flirtations were aired, talked about, and discussed, he was willing to continue on with me if I was. I had finally admitted how much I cared for him, how happy I was to have his name tattooed on my wrist and my name on his wrist, I was happy to have Igor's name removed from my back and to be moving on to a new chapter in my life. I trusted Neel finally, I was forgiving myself for my behaviors of April and early May and I was writing non stop. My kids were angry and confused, mommy was breaking apart the family and I was helpless to tell them otherwise, I couldn't be the person to cause conflict, I couldn't be the woman to tell the kids about their cheating father, their father's betrayals, they had seen me cry so often at home, they had seen me drunk, I wouldn't cause them further distress, let them be angry at me rather than cause confusion. THey were getting a gift of becoming closer to their dad finally after years of him being consumed with video games, weed, and alcohol, and I wasn't going to take that away from them.

July came and with it Neel and I moved to a new stage of our relationship, we were in love, and with love comes talk of the future, I was sober, he doesn't drink, we loved each other so talk of marriage was brought up, he asked me to marry him and I agreed. Too soon or not, I am in love, happy, and finding that love doesn't have to mean punishing, vindictive, hateful behavior, it can be kind, considerate, and sweet. We planned a trip to Northern India to meet his parents, to meet his newborn niece, brother, and sister. I was terrified, I didn't know the customs, I didn't know the language, and I had to meet family. The anxiety was through the roof but it was a great distraction from the fact that I wasn't going to be going back to the US for at least 6 months if not a year, I was abandoning my kids for love, I was abandoning my kids to protect myself from emotional abuse from their father. I was abandoning my kids in favor of myself, that old tale of in order to stay sober we have to take care of ourselves first, before kids, loved ones, family, etc. Sobriety must be number one, and in this case its emotional well being which leads to sobriety must come first, if I'm around the soon to be ex I'll drink or hate myself and drink so I had made the choice to stay.

The trip to Northern India went well, I learned to bow and say Namaste to the future in-laws, I watched as Neel touched feet in respect to his parents and elders, I was greeted, and I greeted those around me, I was sized up, and talked to, I was intimidated and afraid but I kept smiling through it all. I was sober and able to maintain my composure, it was a fun trip that led to being welcomed into my future family. Coming back to Bangalore Neel and I hit a snag in our relationship, I was struggling with Igor, I was upset, and he was worried about my being upset would lead me to flirting with other men, I tried to reassure him but it brought him back to our early beginnings of our relationship, he made comments and suggestions, and I was brought back to the fact of men being assholes, cheaters, and cruel beings, I was devastated, why was I giving up my kids for this guy, why was I willing to do this? Neel and I talked, we talked more, and I told him he needed to choose, could he forgive and move on, or should I book a ticket back to the US, I would be faced with narcissism, manipulation, I would probably drink, but at least I would be with my kids who missed me. We forgive each other, he loved me, he cried for me, he begged me for forgiveness, and I I forgave him, we became closer than ever before.

August came around and with it I was being pressured by Igor, was I coming back to the US, the kids were moving to Florida, he's had to work remotely and his mom was going to move with the kids to Florida, his dad would follow eventually. I have a responsibilit, I'm a mom, I had refused to have an abortion so I need to come home. When I started my life as a kid I've always dreamed of the perfect fairy tale life, I've always wanted to have a big wedding with the perfect wedding dress, I wanted to have the father daughter dance, and be given away by my dad, I wanted to have a small honeymoon before starting married life with my soul mate. I thought I would have 2 kids and a dog around the age of 26 or 30 even, I wanted a career, money in the bank, and I wanted happiness more than anything else. What happened was a shotgun marriage that led to hate, resentment, and cheating, 2 kids that were very much so wanted by me, but only partially liked by the resentful man, 2 dogs one who died after being alive for only 1 year, lots of debt, lots of hate, resentment, and life lessons the biggest being I am allergic to alcohol, when I'm stressed I lean towards bad behaviors that cause me to self destruct. So here I am in the middle of August, I'm abandoning my kids and filled with the knowledge that I'm doing the right thing, my ego says one thing, but my heart says another; I'm the mom of 2 beautiful kids who won't talk to me because all they know is that their mom went to India to be treated for a chronic illness and won't be home for months, she has a boyfriend whom she plans to marry, and she isn't coming home to them. Life is complicated but for today as long as I don't drink, I don't flirt, I don't partake in self destructive behaviors, and I take care of myself I know that one day soon I'll be home to take care of my kids, I'll be home to right the wrongs of my past, and I'll be back to take them to therapy. Today I get to take care of my mind, my heart, my body, and soul, I'm not a slut, I'm not a whore, I'm not a piece of garbage, today I'm worthy, and sometimes that just has to be enough. We all start somewhere, and we all have pieces of our lives that no other human will understand and many will not approve of but the moral of all good stories is simply to live your life and stop letting others thoughts, opinions, and words dictate what your story is supposed to be. You only live once so how are you going to live today? Today I'm going out into the world knowing I'm going to be the best version of myself, I'm sober, I won't drink or use drugs, I won't self destruct, and I will keep reaching out to my kids no matter what. I won't be that person who trash talks about others seeking to put myself on a pedestal, and I will begin planning for a wedding, a future, and to be back in the US to care for my kids. Fear won't hold me back no more!

Made in the USA
Middletown, DE
27 October 2022